CHRISTMAS
ROSES

CHRISTMAS ROSES

AMANDA CABOT

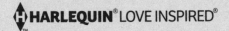

Recycling programs
for this product may
not exist in your area.

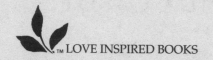

™ LOVE INSPIRED BOOKS

ISBN-13: 978-0-373-78871-2

Christmas Roses

Love Inspired Books/October 2014

First published by Revell, a division of Baker Publishing Group

www.Harlequin.com

For Stephen Joseph Tayntor,
whose questions about his great-grandmother
helped inspire this story. Thanks, Steve!

AMANDA CABOT

Dreams have always been an important part of Amanda Cabot's life. For almost as long as she can remember, she dreamed of being an author. Fortunately for the world, her grade-school attempts as a playwright were not successful, and she turned her attention to writing novels. Her dream of selling a book before her thirtieth birthday came true, and she's been spinning tales ever since. She now has more than twenty-five novels to her credit under a variety of pseudonyms.

Amanda is a member of ACFW, a charter member of Romance Writers of America, and an avid traveler. She married her high school sweetheart, who shares her love of travel and who's driven thousands of miles to help her research her books. A few years ago they fulfilled a longtime dream and are now living in the American West.

Chapter One

October 1882, Wyoming Territory

"Emma needs a father."

"And I need a husband." Celia Anderson sighed as she completed the sentence. It wasn't the first time the parson's wife had pronounced those words. In fact, they were becoming a regular refrain. Celia poured her visitor a cup of coffee, managing a smile as she touched the delicate rose-patterned china that had been her most prized wedding gift. Though they sat in the kitchen so that Celia could watch the children, Bertha Pearson's position in Easton society, not to mention the fact that she was Celia's dearest friend, meant that her coffee was served in china rather than the everyday crockery.

"I know you mean well, Bertha, but I'm

not ready to remarry." She refused to add the thought that had haunted her for the past year. Bertha would only disagree, probably vehemently, if Celia admitted that she wasn't certain she would ever be ready.

She looked around the room where she had spent so many hours since this house had become her home. With an oversized range dominating one wall and a long counter with a sink nestled under the sole window, the kitchen was designed to accommodate a large family or, in Celia's case, a business establishment. The thought that she might have to sell it caused more sleepless nights than Celia could count, but she refused to think about that now. She had a guest to entertain.

"Running the boardinghouse and taking care of Emma and Aaron keep me plenty busy." Aaron, the young child whose father paid Celia to take care of him during the day, looked up and giggled at the sound of his name but soon returned to playing with his blocks, his brown hair falling over his eyes as he concentrated on building a tower. "I don't have time for a husband," Celia added. She feigned a shudder as she said, "All that extra laundry."

Raising both hands in the universal sign for surrender, Bertha conceded the point. "All right." Though gray threaded the auburn locks and she was plumper than fashion demanded, the parson's wife was still a striking woman with her bright hair and green eyes, so different from Celia's own pale blonde tresses and blue eyes. "It's simply that Reverend Pearson and I worry about you." Bertha nodded at Emma, who had fallen asleep in the clothes basket that served as a bassinette. "We want this precious little girl to have everything she deserves, and we think you should be as happy as we are."

"Not all marriages are as happy as yours," Celia said as calmly as she could. Josef had never once looked at her the way Reverend Pearson looked at his wife, as if the world were a much better place, simply because Bertha was there. Celia did not doubt that Josef had cared for her, but caring was not the same thing as love.

"It may have taken you and Josef longer to start a family than some couples, but you were blessed with Emma." A touch of sadness colored Bertha's voice, and she reached for her coffee to disguise her discomfort. Though the Pearsons had been married for thirty years, they were childless, a state that Bertha admitted still pained them.

As if on cue, Celia's little blessing wakened

and began to cough. "She's been crankier than normal this morning with this cough. I think she may have a bit of a fever too." Celia rose to draw her daughter into her arms, crooning softly as she rocked the child. Did all mothers worry as much as she did, or were her concerns magnified by the fact that Emma was her long-awaited child and, in all likelihood, the only one she would have? Celia didn't know. All she knew was that she worried. Though she reminded herself that Emma was a healthy six-month-old girl, she couldn't stop the fears from creeping in when something was even slightly amiss.

"It's probably nothing more than a cold, but I don't think I should go to the meeting." Celia patted Emma's back. "I don't want to disappoint Aaron, though. He's been looking forward to the ride." The women of Easton were all traveling to the neighboring town of Cedarville to plan the two communities' joint Thanksgiving celebration, giving Aaron a rare opportunity to ride in a buggy. Celia raised a questioning eyebrow as she looked at her friend. "Would you take Aaron with you?"

Bertha's smile was little less than a grin, for she loved the youngster as much as Celia did and sought opportunities to spend time with him. "Of course." She took a final swallow of coffee before standing. "Let's get your coat, Aaron. You and I are going for a ride."

"Mrs. Celia?"

When Celia shook her head, the boy's normally sunny face turned bright red as he scrunched his nose and narrowed his eyes. "No!" he wailed. "I wanna stay with Mrs. Celia." It was the prelude to a full-fledged tantrum. Though rare, they were decidedly unpleasant, leaving both Celia and her charge exhausted in the aftermath.

Hoping to forestall the wailing and flailing, Celia took a step closer to Aaron. "I need a big boy to help me," she said, emphasizing the adjective. Tall for his age and as stocky as his father, Aaron was already a big boy, and there were few things he enjoyed more than being reminded of it. "Someone has to go with Mrs. Pearson. You see, I need someone to tell the other ladies I'll bring a pound cake. It's very important."

As she had hoped, Aaron's face returned to its normal color, curiosity replacing rage. "Pound cake. Can you remember that?" When he nodded, Celia patted his shoulder. "Thank you, Aaron. I trust you to deliver my message."

As the boy scampered away to retrieve his coat, Bertha laughed. "No wonder Jacob wants to marry you. You handle Aaron better than Rachel did."

"Nonsense." Celia wasn't certain what bothered her more, the notion of Jacob wanting to marry her or the comparison to his late wife. She wasn't at all like Rachel Bender, and—as she had told Bertha—she wasn't ready to marry Jacob or anyone. "It's simply that Aaron's a year older now. That's why he listens to me." There was nothing to be gained by mentioning that though Rachel had been the most beautiful woman in Easton, she had coddled her son.

As she waved good-bye to Bertha and Aaron, Celia tried not to frown. She didn't want to think about Aaron and his father, especially not today when Emma needed her. Though she'd made light of it to Bertha, the cough worried Celia. Cradling the baby in her arms, she paced slowly from one side of the kitchen to the other. It was only when Emma was once more asleep in her bassinette and Celia was washing the china that the thoughts returned. Though it had started as nothing more than a business transaction—minding Aaron during the day in exchange for some much-needed money—the motherless child had made his way into her heart. But just because she cared deeply for the little boy did not mean Celia wanted to marry his father.

The only reason she had agreed that Aaron and his father, along with Frank Tyson, the owner of Easton's general store, could take supper with her and her boarders was that there were so few boarders. Since Mr. Mortenson had decided that copper mining was not for him and left town two weeks earlier, Celia had only one paying guest. That wasn't enough. The money she earned by feeding the two other men and caring for Aaron helped cover her costs, but only barely. As a result, though she wouldn't admit it to Bertha, there were days when Celia feared that her plan to earn a living by running a boardinghouse was destined for failure.

She dried the second cup, smiling as she always did at the sight of the pink roses apparently blooming around the side. Practical Josef had called the china a shocking waste of money, but Celia had been adamant. When her parents had given her the money they had saved for Celia's wedding, Mama had insisted that it should be spent on something their daughter wanted. Rose-patterned china might be an extravagance, particularly now that she was a widow struggling to pay her bills, but the pretty dishes never failed to boost Celia's spirits.

"I'll find a way," Celia told her sleeping daughter. Was it her imagination that Emma's face seemed more flushed? Perhaps it was the warmth of the kitchen. When she had carefully returned the china to its place in the dining room, Celia left the door open, letting cool air flow into the kitchen.

Even one more boarder would make a big difference, but at this time of the year, it was unlikely anyone would be coming to Easton. Somehow, Celia would have to make do until spring. Though she wished she could confide her worries to Bertha, Celia knew better. The parson's wife would propose her favorite solution: marriage. She would even suggest possible suitors. It was Bertha's theory that Jacob and Frank had asked to take meals here because they harbored romantic notions toward Celia.

That was nonsense. At least Celia thought it was. She had seen no sign of anything resembling affection coming from either of the men, but when she'd mentioned that to Bertha, the older woman had countered by claiming that they were waiting for her year of deep mourning to end. The time of black, as Celia's mother had referred to it, was over. It had been thirteen months since Josef had been killed bringing copper out of the mine, more than six months since Emma's birth. Celia's life was settled, and if it wasn't perfect, well…a husband wasn't the answer.

Two hours later she hoisted Emma into her high chair, frowning a little when the child began to cough again. "Dinner's ready, sweetie. I made your favorite: peas." But though Emma normally relished the mashed vegetable, today she batted at the spoon and refused to open her mouth other than to cough.

Celia frowned again. There was no doubt about it. The cough was worse. Though she had hoped that the morning nap would cure it, it had not. Celia gathered her daughter into her arms and walked the few steps to the storage room that she'd turned into Emma's daytime nursery, settling into the rocking chair. Rocking was the one thing she was certain would calm Emma, but even that failed, and it took a full hour before Emma drifted off to sleep.

With a quick look at her watch, Celia hurried upstairs. Today was the day she changed her boarders' sheets. Normally she completed that task soon after breakfast, but Bertha's visit and Emma's crankiness had kept her downstairs. The sole good thing she could say about having only one boarder was that it would take her no more than a few minutes to clean his room.

She hurried, filled by an urgency she couldn't explain, and it was less than ten minutes later that she descended the stairs, dirty sheets in her arms.

Croak! The sound came from Emma. Dropping the sheets, Celia raced back into the storage room. For a second she stood motionless, shocked by the sight of her daughter with a horribly flushed face.

Emma's cry was sharp and shrill, punctuated by another croaking cough.

"Oh, Emma!" Celia swept her baby into her arms, patting her on the back in a vain attempt to stop her coughing. "What's wrong, sweetie?" In response, Emma took another shallow breath before emitting that dreadful croaking sound. "Oh, Emma!" Celia sank onto the chair, then opened her daughter's mouth. Perhaps she had somehow put an object into her mouth and that was causing the choking sounds. But Emma's mouth was empty, and her throat showed no sign of inflammation.

As another cough racked her daughter's frame, Celia's arms began to tremble with fear. This was no simple cold. A cold didn't cause a cough like this. A cold didn't make a child's breathing labored. Something was terribly wrong. Celia bit her lip to avoid crying out. She had to help Emma, but what could she do? The doctor had been called into the hills to help an old hermit. The other women were all in Cedarville, planning the Thanksgiving celebration. Celia was on her own with no idea how to help her suffering child.

"Emma, sweetie, I love you." She crooned the words as she rocked her baby, trying to remember what her mother had done when she had a cough. Vaguely she recalled honey in tea, but Bertha had said babies weren't supposed to eat honey. As she eyed a jar of honey, Celia shook her head. Even if it wouldn't harm her, Emma was coughing so badly that it was unlikely she would be able to swallow anything.

If she hadn't closed her ears when the other women had spoken of their children's ailments, not wanting to be reminded that she had no babies of her own, she would know what to do. Now she was helpless. Celia had lost Josef, and thanks to her stubborn pride, she might lose their daughter.

Help me, Lord. Save my baby.

Mark Williams reined in his horse, pausing at the top of the rise to look at the small town. It had been two years, three months, seventeen days, and more miles and towns than he could count. Each time, the lead he followed had seemed promising. Each time, it had turned into a dead end. While it seemed unlikely that the man he sought would have come to a copper mining town in eastern Wyoming, that was the only lead Mark had, and so here he was, staring at a village that couldn't boast more than 150 people. Nestled in a small valley, Easton consisted of one main street with a couple tracks that could hardly be dignified with the term "street" leading off to the east. From his position on the rise, it appeared that the majority of the buildings were of frame construction, although the one with the steeple was white stone, perhaps the same limestone he'd seen at Fort Laramie.

"C'mon, Charcoal." Mark leaned forward and patted his horse's neck. For more than two years, Charcoal had been his only friend, listening to him grumble about the dead ends while he carried Mark and a pair of panniers laden with tools from town to town. "We might as well see if the old man is here." The Kansas wheat farmer who had scratched his head in amazement that someone had come looking for Abe Williams after all those years had claimed that Abe had headed West when he heard there were fortunes to be made in Colorado and Wyoming. "Just as well," the farmer had told Mark. "Abe was a right friendly one, but he weren't cut out for farming. I don't reckon he cared for it."

Or for fathering. Mark wouldn't think about that now. There'd be time enough to hear the excuses once he found the man who'd abandoned his wife and newborn son. To distract himself from the thoughts that still caused his stomach to clench, Mark studied the town he was approaching. It was more attractive than he'd thought, except for the gash in the earth that marked the entrance to the mine. Nothing could make that pretty, but the buildings were well cared for, despite the copper-colored dust that marred once-pristine paint finishes. There was no escaping dust with the Wyoming wind. Mark suspected that it permeated just about everything, leaving its characteristic color in every crease and wrinkle of a man's face and giving all the women's hair a reddish tinge.

He had no opportunity to judge the validity of that supposition, for the main street was emptier than he'd expected. At this time of day, women often strolled a town's streets, visiting friends or shopping at the mercantile. Today, however, Easton seemed almost deserted. Judging from the sound of metal clanking, the livery was in operation, and what appeared to be the only store in town was open, its plate-glass window filled with an array of goods designed to attract shoppers. A fancy hat perched next to a pair of sturdy boots might lure adults, while half a dozen marbles spilling from a bag would appeal to youngsters.

With Charcoal tethered to the hitching post, Mark entered the general store, pausing to let his eyes adjust to the darkness. That was one thing about Wyoming. The sky was brighter and bluer than anywhere he'd been. And, though there was no denying its beauty, there were times it almost hurt a man's eyes.

"Can I help you, sir?" A boy Mark guessed to be no more than twelve or thirteen came out from behind the counter, the curiosity in his expression suggesting that visitors were rare.

"I'm looking for a place to stay." Perhaps he should have asked about his father first. That's what he'd always done when he'd entered a new place, but something—perhaps fear of what he would learn—held him back. It was midafternoon, Mark reasoned. Even if Abe Williams was here, chances were good he was working in the mine, and that meant he wouldn't be aboveground for hours, perhaps not even before the sunset. There was no way around it. Mark would be staying here tonight, and though he had spent countless nights sleeping under the stars, he preferred a bed. He'd find one, then look for Abe.

The boy shook his head. "We ain't got no hotel, but you might wanna talk to Widow Anderson. She opened a boardinghouse back ten or eleven months ago, and everybody knows it ain't full. I reckon she'd let you stay for a night or two."

When Mark raised an eyebrow in a silent request for directions, the boy continued. "You cain't miss it. It's the biggest house in town. Just follow the road. It's on the right side."

The boy had not exaggerated. The boardinghouse that appeared to be the last sign of civilization before the street turned into a narrow trail that disappeared into the forest was at least three times the size of the other houses in Easton. The only two-story building in town, it had a mansard roof and was graced with a wraparound porch. A swing twice as long as the one where his mother had read him stories creaked in the wind, the reddish dust on its seat telling Mark it had been days since anyone had relaxed there. And that was a shame, because the swing had a view of one of the prettiest landscapes Mark had encountered. Though the deciduous trees had shed their leaves, the hills were dotted with the deep green of junipers and pines, interspersed with the unmistakable gray-green of sagebrushes, all framed by that brilliant blue sky. No one would mistake this for the Ohio farm where he'd grown up, yet there was something about this little town that reminded Mark of home.

Perhaps that was what had drawn Abe here. Mark frowned as he dismounted. It was difficult to imagine his father choosing to spend days underground. In the years he'd spent searching for him, Mark had discovered that Abe Williams had worked on a barge plying the Mississippi. He'd herded cattle in Texas, panned for silver in Colorado, and farmed in Kansas. There had been a dozen other stops along the way. Different states and territories, different occupations. The one constant was that everything had involved being outdoors. The picture Mark had formed was of a man who loved adventure and who would try almost anything...except settling down or being cooped up indoors. If his father wouldn't even work as a blacksmith, mining must be unbearable. Had desperation driven him here, or hadn't he realized what copper mining entailed? By this time tomorrow, Mark would have his answers. He'd know whether Abe Williams was living in Easton. In the meantime, he needed to arrange for a room and board and get Charcoal settled in at the livery.

After tying Charcoal to the front porch, Mark climbed the four steps and knocked on the door. No answer. "Mrs. Anderson?" His call elicited the same response: silence. Perhaps the proprietor had stepped out. Feeling more than a little awkward, Mark turned the knob and pushed the door open, frowning when he noticed that it had settled, causing it to stick. A minute with a plane would fix that.

"Mrs. Anderson?" He took a few steps into what was obviously the parlor of a woman who liked roses. The walls were papered with a pattern of large overblown roses; someone had stitched a circlet of roses on the footstool, and the china vase that stood on a small table was decorated with a perfect red rosebud. No one was in the room. Remembering the empty street and store, Mark wondered if the women of the town might be engaged in a quilting bee or some other female pursuit.

And then he heard it: a painful cough and an even more alarming shrill cry. Following the sounds through the dining room and kitchen, he found himself in a small room. The stacks of canned goods lining one wall would have made him call it a storage room, were it not for the presence of an oak rocking chair and a laundry basket lined with soft blankets. Bemused by the unexpected furnishings, Mark stared at the most beautiful young woman he'd ever seen, a woman who was cradling a desperately ill child.

He guessed her to be in her midtwenties, perhaps a year or two less than his own twenty-six. With hair as golden as a ripe ear of corn and eyes as deep a blue as the Wyoming sky, her face would have been one to fuel a man's dreams were it not for the panic that drained it of all color. Where was Widow Anderson, and why wasn't she helping her boarder care for this child? The baby's face was alarmingly red, and the cough that wracked its body tore at Mark's heart.

"Help me!" the woman cried, her eyes moving frantically from Mark to the child in her arms. "Help my baby! She can't breathe." Though the woman's voice was shrill with fear, Mark detected a slight accent, as if English were her second language.

"Where's the doctor?" Mark had learned a thing or two about emergency care during his travels, but he was no substitute for a trained physician.

"He's gone. Everyone's gone."

That left Mark, and judging from the baby's

labored breathing and the peculiar cough, there was no time to lose. "Where's your vinegar?"

The woman stared at him as if he'd lost his senses but gestured toward a jug on the floor.

"Your daughter needs vinegar steam." As he'd traveled, Mark had seen the difference humidity made. While some claimed that the desert cured many ailments, there were other problems, including coughs like this, that benefited from extremely moist environments. "I'm going to boil water and make a tent for you."

The mother appeared confused, as if she'd never heard of a steam tent. It didn't matter. That was the only thing Mark knew to do when someone had trouble breathing. If his suppositions were correct and this was croup, the vinegar would relieve the congestion or whatever it was that was causing the horrible cough and the labored breathing. "I'll call you when I'm ready," he promised. "Just hold your baby."

Though the woman's lips moved, no sound came out, and Mark suspected she was praying. That couldn't hurt, but a doctor would be better.

He hurried back into the kitchen and looked around. Thank goodness the kettle was filled with water. He'd need more, but this would get them started. While he waited for the water to boil, he searched for a tub to hold it and something to serve as the tent. Though he'd hoped for blankets, the pile of sheets that he found on the floor in the laundry room would have to do. He'd use the kitchen worktable as his platform.

"All right. Bring your daughter into the kitchen," Mark said when he'd arranged everything. He pointed toward the stool he'd placed next to the table. "I want you to sit here and hold her over the water. Keep her face as close to the steam as you can." When the woman was settled, he draped the sheet over her and the baby. Though the pungent smell of vinegar filled the room, he didn't know whether he had added enough. Only time would tell. "I'll start more water heating."

Mark lost count of the number of times he emptied the tub and refilled it with steaming water. Each time he worked the handle on the old pump, he hoped it would remain attached, for there was no time to repair it today. Each time he placed another piece of wood inside the stove, he hoped it would be the last one he needed, for the supply was dwindling. And each time he pulled back the sheets to empty and refill the tub, he looked at the child, searching for a sign that the treatment was working.

It was odd. He ought to be tired. Even before he'd arrived in Easton, it had been a long day, for he'd left well before dawn and had ridden hard to reach the small town. But now he felt no fatigue, nothing but the sensation that he was more alive than he'd been in years, perhaps ever.

Though the mother said little, Mark saw the lines on her face begin to ease as the afternoon passed. She had noticed what he had, that the coughing spells seemed less frequent and less intense. It was perhaps an hour later that the woman smiled. "She's breathing normally," she said, pushing the now-soggy sheets aside. She rose and held the child in her arms, this time cradling her rather than suspending her over the tub. The baby's face was still rosy, but the alarming flush had faded. "I don't know how to thank you," the mother said, her voice husky with emotion. "You were the answer to prayer."

Mark blinked. It was the first time anyone had called him the answer to anything, especially prayer.

"You saved my baby." Celia's arms shook so badly she could barely hold Emma. It wasn't simply the strain of the hours she had spent keeping her suspended over the steaming tub that had taken its toll on her. Somehow the aftermath seemed worse, draining every ounce of strength from her, leaving her as limp as an overcooked carrot.

The stranger looked at her with gray eyes that seemed to understand. "Here, let me hold her. Why don't you sit down?" He gestured toward a chair on the opposite side of the table. Unlike the stool where she'd been perched for hours, it had a back to support her.

As she sank onto the chair, Celia stared at the man who'd arrived at the exact moment she had needed him. She had always pictured angels as blond and cherubic, with plump cheeks and sweet smiles, but no one would have described this man as a cherub. He was tall, with hair so dark it was almost black and eyes the color of smoke. His angular face with its roughly chiseled features bore no resemblance to Celia's mental image, and yet there was no doubt that he was the answer to her prayer, an angel in human form. "God sent you," Celia said, marveling at the perfect timing.

The way the stranger cleared his throat told her he was uncomfortable, although whether it was by her reference to God or the implied praise wasn't clear. "I wouldn't say that, ma'am," he said, keeping his eyes fixed on Emma rather than meeting Celia's gaze. "I was just passing through town. I needed a place to stay, and the boy at the mercantile told me Widow Anderson might have a room." This time he directed his look at her. "Do you know where she is?"

A bubble of laughter escaped from Celia's mouth. This was no coincidence. God had definitely sent the man to her. She had prayed for another boarder, but he had sent something even better: a boarder who knew how to heal a child. "I'm Celia Anderson," she said, "and my daughter is Emma." It was strange. They had worked together, battling for Emma's life, and yet she didn't know the man's name.

"You're welcome to stay here," she told him. "In fact, I insist that you stay—rent free, of course. It's the least I can do after all you've done for us, Mr...." Celia let her voice trail off, hoping he'd complete the sentence.

"Williams. Mark Williams. It's true I need a room, but I don't want to impose on you, especially today." He looked down at Emma, who had fallen asleep, probably exhausted by her ordeal.

"Nonsense. This is a boardinghouse, and I have plenty of room. There are six bedchambers upstairs, and only one is occupied." Celia rose and took Emma from his arms. "Let me put her to bed, and then I'll show you your room."

There was no question of which one she would give Mr. Williams. Five minutes later, Celia led him upstairs and opened the door to her largest guest chamber. Situated on the front corner above the dining room, it had windows on two sides, providing a view of both the street and the forest.

Mr. Williams nodded as he looked around. "I'm much obliged, ma'am. This is nicer than anywhere I've slept in years."

And far less than he deserved. "Get yourself settled and then come downstairs. I'll fix you a cup of coffee and some *pepparkakor*."

"Pepper what?"

"*Pepparkakor*. I can tell you're not Swedish. Those are the best spice cookies you'll ever taste. Every woman in Sweden tries to outdo her neighbors, but no one's recipe can compare to my grandmother's." Celia shook her head. "Here I am, bragging about cookies instead of making sure you're comfortable." She looked around, satisfying herself that she had left fresh towels on the bureau. She'd fill the pitcher later. "If there's anything you need, Mr. Williams, just let me know."

"There is something," he said, his eyes lightening as he smiled. "I'd appreciate it if you'd call me Mark. Where I come from, we're not set on formality."

The request was highly unconventional. Although she was on a first-name basis with the women in town and with her boarders, she referred to other men as "mister." Still, Mr. Williams would be here only a day or two. What harm could it cause?

"Certainly, Mark." She gave him a small smile. "And you may call me Celia."

Ten minutes later, she heard his footsteps on the stairway and met him at the base. "Please, have a seat in the parlor." It was her favorite room of the house, filled as it was with reminders of the flowers she had loved from early childhood. When they were both seated and she'd served him the coffee and cookies she had promised, Celia cleared her throat. She had to let him know how much she appreciated his actions. "I wish there were a way I could thank you for what you did this afternoon. I don't know what I would have done without you." Yes, she did. She would have lost Emma. "You must have children of your own."

Mark's eyebrows rose, and he shook his

head. "'Fraid not. I'm a bachelor and likely to remain that way."

"Then you have younger siblings."

He shook his head again. "Nope. What makes you think I've been surrounded by children?"

"The way you knew what to do and the ease with which you held Emma. Few men are that comfortable around babies."

Mark took a sip of coffee before he replied. "I've been traveling for the past two years, ever since Ma died. Along the way, I learned to do a lot of things, including caring for sick babies."

Celia wondered where he'd learned that particular skill, but she wouldn't ask. If there was one lesson Mama had taught her, it was not to pry into others' lives. She had already asked too many personal questions.

Mark nodded when she offered him another cookie, then said, "I never saw croup before, but I've heard about it."

"Croup." Remembering the tiny graves in the cemetery that Bertha claimed were the result of croup, Celia shuddered. Were it not for this man, her daughter might have died. "Are you sure you're not a doctor?"

"No doctor, just an itinerant carpenter."

Chapter Two

He had planned to start his inquiries as soon as he'd found a room, but he hadn't wanted to leave Celia and Emma. Though he thought the crisis had passed, you could never be certain with an illness, and so Mark had decided to postpone his search. After more than two years, another day made no difference. The child was sleeping better now. She still coughed, but the alarming croaking had subsided, and Celia reported that her face was no longer flushed. There was nothing more for Mark to do, and so he sat in the parlor, trying not to wince at the rose motifs. It wasn't that he disliked the flower. The ones Ma had in her garden had smelled better than any of the other plants. It was simply that there were so many of them in this room.

When the front door opened and a middle-aged man entered the house, Mark felt a jolt of energy. Celia had told him to expect three men and a young boy for dinner but had said nothing more.

"You a new boarder?" The man who tossed his jacket onto the coatrack was a couple inches shorter than Mark with brown eyes and what would probably be medium brown hair, once it dried. It and his face and hands had obviously just been washed, leaving Mark with the impression that the man was a miner who'd sought to wash off the telltale dust.

Mark rose, extending his hand in greeting. "I'm just passing through. Name's Mark Williams."

"Hiram Dinkel here." The man gave him an appraising look. "Sure is a shame you're not staying. Celia—that is, Mrs. Anderson—could use more boarders. I'm the only one." He frowned slightly as he settled onto the horsehair chair that boasted a pillow embroidered with pink roses, but whether the frown was caused by the floral design or his thoughts wasn't clear. "She don't say much, but I reckon it's been mighty hard on her, losin' her man and then tryin' to make a go of this place. Don't know whether she told you, but she bought this place soon after Josef got killed.

Folks figured she was crazy, tryin' to make a livin' by herself, but she's a plucky one."

Mark nodded. Hiram's story explained the boardinghouse's lack of repairs. Celia probably couldn't afford them, especially if she had only one boarder. "This looks like a nice town, but like I said, I'm just passing through." Since the man appeared friendly, Mark decided to start his inquiry with him. "I'm looking for someone. You ever hear of Abe Williams?"

Furrows formed between Hiram Dinkel's eyes. "Williams, huh? Family?" When Mark nodded, he continued. "Can't say as I recognize the name. There ain't no one by that name at the mine, but you oughta ask the others. Could be they've met him. He mighta been here before I came. Frank or Jacob would know. They oughta be here any—"

Before Hiram could complete the sentence, the door burst open and a boy Mark guessed to be no older than three launched himself into the room. "Mrs. Celia! Mrs. Celia! I found the ladies. I did just like you said."

Celia emerged from the kitchen, a voluminous white apron covering her dress. Mark noticed that she'd combed her hair since Emma's ordeal, and tendrils no longer escaped from the coronet of braids. Her face was flushed, but he suspected that was the result of rushing around a warm kitchen rather than a sign of illness.

Celia bent down to ruffle the boy's hair as she said, "Thank you, Aaron. I knew I could count on you." When the child grinned in pleasure, she turned her attention to the two men who'd followed him into the parlor. "Good evening, gentlemen. Have you met Mark Williams? He'll be staying for a day or two. Now, if you'll excuse me, I need to finish supper."

Mark looked at the two newcomers, both of whom were heavier than Hiram. The brown-haired man in overalls, who merely nodded in greeting, bore a striking resemblance to Aaron and was presumably his father. The other man, heavy, blond-haired, and dressed in a suit, stepped forward. "You must be the stranger Daniel told me about. He said he'd sent you this way." The look on the man's face told Mark that, unlike Hiram, this man didn't seem to think Celia needed another boarder, even for a short time. "I'm Frank Tyson," he said. "That's my mercantile you visited." He thrust his shoulders back, as if asserting his importance in Easton, and the look he gave Mark was anything but friendly.

"It looked like a fine establishment." Mark knew the value of honeyed words in soothing an antagonist. "That's good for me, because I need to stock up on a few things before I leave."

Apparently mollified, Frank nodded. "I've got most anything you could want. Isn't that right, Jacob?"

The other man stepped forward, bending slightly to place his hand on the boy's head. "Welcome to Easton, Mr. Williams. I'm Jacob Bender. This here's my son, Aaron."

"I help Mrs. Celia," the child announced.

The pride in his brown eyes reminded Mark of himself as a youngster, always trying to please his mother. "She's lucky to have a big boy to help her."

As if on cue, Celia reentered the parlor, this time without her apron. "Supper's ready," she said, taking Aaron's hand as she led the way into the dining room. When Mark had walked through here before, the table had been bare. Now it was covered with a cloth and laden with six place settings and three large platters of food.

Once inside the room, Aaron scampered to the high chair on one side of the table. While his father helped him into it, Hiram walked to one of the two seats on the opposite side, leaving the one next to the high chair vacant for Jacob. Frank, however, stood in the doorway, staring at the table. As if she sensed his confusion, Celia moved to the foot of the table and nodded toward the empty seat between her and Hiram. "You'll be in your usual spot, Frank. Mark, I've placed you at the other end."

"Harrumph." Though Frank pulled out Celia's chair, he made no effort to disguise his displeasure that Mark had been assigned the seat at the head of the table. Clearly Frank thought he deserved it. It was silly, really. Given the choice, Mark would have preferred to sit beside Celia rather than between Hiram and Jacob, but Frank had other ideas.

"My apologies, gentlemen," Celia said when Frank had offered a blessing for the food. "I know you were expecting a hot meal, but Emma was very ill today, and I had no time to cook." Though he had attributed no importance to it, Mark saw that the platters were of cold meats, cheeses, and breads. It might not be hot, but it appeared to be the best meal he'd had in a week.

As he passed the cheeses to Mark, Hiram's brown eyes radiated concern. "Is Emma all right now?"

"Much better." Celia gave her boarder a smile. "Doc Rudinski was gone, but Mr. Williams knew what to do. If it weren't for him, Emma might not be alive."

Turning to Mark, Hiram nodded. "I reckon the good Lord sent you here at the right time."

Before Mark could tell him that he and the good Lord were not on speaking terms and that the only place God was likely to send him was considerably warmer than Wyoming Territory, Celia spoke. "That's what I said."

"So, why did you come here?" It was Frank who asked the question, his voice holding a hint of belligerence and something that sounded like jealousy.

Mark washed down a bite of meat with a drink of water. "I'm looking for a man—Abe Williams. Hiram said he doesn't work at the mine now, but he thought you and Jacob might recognize the name."

At the other end of the table, Celia buttered a slice of bread, those deep blue eyes thoughtful. Jacob shook his head. "I've been here since the mine opened, and I can't recall anyone by that name."

"He might have just been passing through." Like me, Mark wanted to add. Since he'd left Ohio, the longest he'd stayed anywhere had been a month, and only then because he'd needed to earn enough money to get him to his next destination.

"My memory's sharper than most." If he'd been a rooster, Frank would have puffed out his chest feathers. "I never heard of anybody by that name. Could be he used an assumed name, though. Some folks do." Frank snagged another piece of roast beef. "What's he look like?"

The answer was easy. "Me. He's my pa."

Though Mark had thought Aaron was so engrossed in creating meat and cheese balls to accompany the ones he'd constructed of bread that he had paid no attention to the conversation, the boy piped up. "How come your pa ain't with you? My pa's right here."

Out of the mouths of babes. Aaron had asked the question that had plagued Mark ever since he'd learned his father was still alive. There was no answer, so he said only, "Some pas are different."

"If I were you, I'd ask the parson." Frank helped himself to another serving of cheese before reaching for the bread. "Reverend Pearson knows most everybody in the area, not just Easton."

As she sliced a pickle, Celia said, "Cedarville—that's the next town—doesn't have a minister of its own, so Reverend Pearson serves them too. If your father's been here in the last twenty years, Reverend Pearson will know."

"I'll visit him first thing in the morning."

When the men had finished eating, Celia cleared the plates, then stood in the doorway to the kitchen, a coffeepot in her hand. "Would you gentlemen like some cookies with your coffee? I have *pepparkakor*."

His mouth watering at the thought of the delicious sweets, Mark nodded. "They're mighty tasty."

In unison, Frank's and Jacob's heads swiveled, and they glared at Mark, plainly annoyed that he had sampled the cookies before them. Their behavior was so juvenile that Mark almost laughed, and yet part of him understood. Though they might not have declared their intent, both men clearly had a romantic interest in Celia, and neither liked the idea of another man being near her, even if that man was only passing through. He couldn't blame them. Celia was beautiful, a devoted mother, and, if the cookies and bread were any indication, an excellent cook. If Mark were the marrying kind, she would be the type of woman he would favor.

If he were the marrying kind.

Celia's eyes fluttered open, and for the briefest of moments, she stared, bemused by the white light that seeped around the edges of the shades. Snow. There was no mistaking the way it changed the world, hiding the copper dust, replacing it with a blanket of white. As she rolled over to glance at the clock, she gasped. She'd overslept. Though Emma's fever had subsided and the cough diminished, she had been restless for most of the night, and it had been late before Celia had fallen asleep. Now she was behind schedule. Hurriedly, she splashed water on her face and slipped into a morning gown, grateful that it did not require a corset. Once the men left, she would take the time to dress properly. In the meantime, she had breakfast to prepare.

Unwilling to leave Emma, even though the child was sleeping peacefully, Celia lifted the basket and carried her daughter into the kitchen. And there she found the second surprise of the morning. The wood box was full, and a bucket of water sat on the counter next to the sink. Someone had taken care of the most pressing chores. Thanks to her Good Samaritan, she could have breakfast ready at the normal time.

As she cracked eggs into a large bowl, Celia smiled. It had to be Mark who'd helped her. Hiram was a kind man, but it would never have occurred to him to do women's work. When the eggs were scrambled and the bacon fried, Celia walked to the foot of the stairs and called the men. Mark descended first, his face still damp from his morning ablutions. Though he wore a clean shirt and pair of pants, both were so wrinkled that Celia resolved to do his laundry. It would be small recompense for all he'd given her and Emma.

"I found fresh water and wood in the kitchen," Celia said when Mark reached her side. "Do I have you to thank?"

He shrugged, as if the effort were of no account. "I did it last night. I was afraid Emma might have a setback and we'd need it."

Celia wasn't certain what warmed her heart more, Mark's thoughtfulness or his use of the plural pronoun. "Again, I don't know how to thank you."

"It was nothing."

When another shrug accompanied his words, Celia shook her head. "It was something to me. Thank you."

Half an hour later, the men were gone, Hiram headed for the mine, Mark to visit the parson. Celia had changed into the dark skirt and white shirtwaist that were her normal daytime attire and was back in the kitchen, washing dishes while she waited for Jacob to bring Aaron.

"Good morning, Celia." Bertha's voice carried through the house. "What happened to your door?"

Celia turned, startled by the unexpected question. "What do you mean?" she asked as her friend entered the kitchen.

Though Bertha was clad in her normal somber gray, her face was reddened by the cold, and she chafed her hands to warm them. "Your door opened properly," she said, a hint of surprise in her voice. "You know how it always sticks. Well, it didn't this morning."

A rush of pleasure flooded Celia's veins. "It must have been Mark, my temporary boarder."

"Mark?" Surprise turned to disapproval, highlighted by Bertha's raised eyebrow. "Isn't that a bit familiar?"

Under ordinary circumstances Celia would have agreed, but yesterday had been anything but ordinary. "He asked me to address him that way," she told Bertha, wishing she didn't feel the need to explain. "Besides, he's only going to be here for another day or so. He's on his way to see the reverend right now."

Bertha took the chair Celia offered and nodded when she lifted the coffeepot. "What do you know about him?"

"Other than the fact that he saved Emma's life and is looking for his father, not much. Oh yes, he chopped wood for me, brought in water, and fixed my front door." A hint of asperity tinged Celia's words, but Bertha didn't seem to notice. She focused on one part of Celia's explanation.

"Saved Emma's life? What do you mean?"

Celia explained, concluding with what seemed to be becoming a refrain. "I'm convinced the Lord sent him."

Bertha appeared less convinced. "That may be, but you need to be careful. A woman alone cannot be too vigilant."

"Yes, Mama." Celia accompanied her words with a crooked smile, hoping to deflect Bertha's attention. If not, she'd start her lecture about Emma needing a father and Celia needing a husband. Bertha meant well, but sometimes she could be like a robin with a worm, unwilling to give up once she started tugging. The truth was, Celia didn't need a husband. Still, if she were putting in an order for one, she would ask for a man who'd love her and Emma so much that he'd chop wood, bring water, and fix the door, all without being asked. A man like Mark Williams.

Mark found himself whistling as he headed south on Main Street. It was as close to a perfect day as he could recall. The snow sparkled like diamonds, the air was redolent with the smell of cedars and junipers, and his heart was filled with satisfaction. It had been a simple task to fix Celia's front door, requiring little more time than oiling the pump had, and yet his sense of achievement at seeing the door open and close without sticking was out of all proportion to the effort he'd expended. Mark had assisted other women along his travels, but nothing had felt as good as helping Celia. She was a special woman, one of a kind.

Mark knocked on the door to the simple log cabin that served as Easton's parsonage. The man who opened the door was tall and thin almost to the point of being gaunt, his dark brown hair liberally threaded with gray, and yet his most distinguishing characteristic was his eyes. Chocolate brown, they appeared to see deep inside a man. It should have been a disconcerting experience, being on the receiving end of that gaze, but Mark found it oddly comforting, as if the parson were dispensing a sense of well-being while he scrutinized his visitor.

"Reverend Pearson?" Mark asked.

"I'm Andrew Pearson. How may I help you?" His voice was deep and resonant, what Mark had always called a preacher's voice.

Shaking the extended hand, he introduced himself. "I arrived in town yesterday and am staying with Mrs. Anderson." He wouldn't refer to her as Celia, not to this man who saw more than most.

The minister ushered Mark into the front room and gestured toward one of the straight-backed chairs. "Ah yes. I heard we had a visitor."

Mark suspected he'd heard more than the simple fact of his arrival. Frank and Jacob hadn't struck him as silent types, and it wouldn't surprise him if one of them had paid a call on the minister. "You might have heard that I'm looking for my father, Abe Williams."

Rather than confirm Mark's supposition, the reverend fixed him with another piercing gaze. "Abe Williams, you say." He looked into the distance for a moment, and lines formed between his eyes. "I'm afraid I haven't heard that name," he said at length.

"Have you seen this man? He'd be older now, of course." Mark unwrapped the oilskin packet that held his only link to his father and pulled out his parents' wedding portrait.

Reverend Pearson studied it carefully before shaking his head. "It seems you've hit a dead end."

Disappointment speared Mark. Even though he'd thought it unlikely that his father had worked as a miner, ever since he'd entered

Easton, he had hoped he was wrong. He had wanted this to be the place he found Abe Williams, the place where his journey ended. But it was nothing more than another dead end.

"Where will you go now?" The parson seemed genuinely interested.

"I'm not sure. This was my last lead. In the past, there was always someone who remembered my father and who knew where he planned to go next. Now…I don't know what to do." He'd lost count of the towns he'd visited, the leads he'd followed. It was enough that he'd kept track of the days he'd spent searching for his father. Each time there had been hope, but now there was none.

His eyes filled with compassion, Reverend Pearson nodded slowly. "I'll pray that you find your way. In the meantime, if you plan to stay in the area, Cedarville has a small hotel. You might be more comfortable there."

Though his voice was neutral, Mark suspected that the minister was encouraging him to leave Easton. "Thank you, but I'm comfortable here. I have no intention of leaving until the doctor says Emma is fully recovered. I'm concerned about her."

Reverend Pearson raised an eyebrow, as if questioning Mark's veracity. "My concern is for her mother. Mrs. Anderson is a beautiful woman, but she's also vulnerable. She doesn't deserve to have anyone trifle with her affections."

It was Mark's turn to nod. "I understand, sir." He not only understood, he was reassured by the knowledge that Celia had such a staunch champion. The minister was being protective, and unlike Frank and Jacob, his feelings were paternal. Mark respected that. "I assure you, I'm no threat to her affections. I'm just passing through."

Chapter Three

"Heard you needed me, Miz Anderson." Doctor Rudinski, whom most people in Easton simply called Doc, removed his hat, revealing sandy blond hair. "Hermit up in the hills had a bad spell. Took longer than I expected." His light blue eyes catalogued Celia's features. "'Pears you've recovered from whatever ailed you."

The doctor was noted for his direct, sometimes abbreviated speech. Though some in Easton considered him curt, Celia knew him to be a compassionate and competent physician. He'd tried his best to save Josef, but the runaway mine cart had crushed her husband's body so badly that only a miracle could have saved him. There had been no miracles that day.

"I wasn't ill," Celia said as she led the doctor into the kitchen where Emma and Aaron were playing. "It was Emma."

When she finished explaining what had happened, Doc nodded. "Sounds like the croup. Mighty dangerous." He peered into Emma's throat and listened to her heartbeat. "You were lucky, Miz Anderson. Quick thinking saved your daughter's life."

That's what she believed too. Having Mark appear when he had was as close to a miracle as Celia had experienced. "I didn't do anything. You know how healthy Emma's been." Doc nodded. "I wasn't prepared for something serious. The truth is, I was practically paralyzed with fear. Mr. Williams was the one who insisted that steam and vinegar were what Emma needed."

Doc raised an eyebrow. "Exactly right. Oughta get him to stay. I sure could use an assistant."

It wasn't a bad idea, but Celia doubted Mark would agree. "I expect him to leave tomorrow or the next day. He claims he's an itinerant carpenter, not a healer."

Doc took one final look at Emma before placing her back on the floor.

"Be that as it may, I still want to meet him."

Celia looked outside, surprised when she saw no sign of Mark. "He went to visit Reverend Pearson. I thought he would have been back by now."

"Oh, well." The doctor closed his medical bag and headed toward the door. "Another time."

It was midafternoon and Celia, who never sang, found herself singing to herself as she prepared dinner. The hen that would become the foundation for tonight's chicken and dumplings was stewing; bread was rising; and she had just taken two chess pies from the oven. As if the delicious aromas perfuming her kitchen weren't enough reason to give thanks, soon after the doctor had left, Emma had sat up by herself, her face wreathed in a grin that said she was proud as could be of her accomplishment. Emma was sitting up again, watching Aaron as he made a tower of blocks. But the primary reason Celia was singing with joy was the sound of hammering and sawing that came from her storeroom.

When he'd returned from visiting the minister, Mark had admitted that Reverend Pearson had been unable to help him. "I'll be leaving soon," he said, "but there's something I want to do first." Though it was clear that Mark was building something, he wouldn't give Celia even a hint of what it was.

"I want your gift to be a surprise," he said, insisting she stay in the parlor while he brought in the materials. It was only when everything was secreted in the storage room and the door closed that Mark allowed Celia back in the kitchen. Even though she had protested that a present wasn't necessary, she had smiled at the prospect of a surprise. There hadn't been many of them in her life, at least not pleasant ones, so the anticipation was as much of a gift as the surprise itself would be.

She was measuring out the ingredients for the dumplings when the sounds from the storeroom stopped and the door opened. Unable to contain her curiosity, Celia glanced in that direction and saw Mark carrying a bag out the back door. The clank of metal on metal suggested the contents were his tools. Only moments later, he strode into the kitchen.

"Are you ready for your surprise?"

Frowning at her flour-covered hands, Celia shook her head. "Give me a minute." It took less than that to wash and dry her hands. "I'm ready now." Ready and as excited as a child on Christmas morning.

Mark held out his arm, bending it so she could place her hand on it. It was a gesture out of a storybook, too formal for men in Easton, and that made it all the more special.

Though she was nothing more than an ordinary woman, a mother trying to make a living for herself and her daughter, Mark was treating Celia as if she were a princess from a fairy tale.

Aaron looked up from the precariously perched pile of blocks that he'd constructed. "I go?"

"Of course." Mark smiled at the boy, then glanced at Emma, who was watching them with apparent interest. "We'll bring Emma too." He wrinkled his nose as he gently disengaged Celia's hand from his arm. "One second. Well, maybe two." Lifting Emma from the floor, he nestled her in the corner of one arm before bending the other for Celia.

As they approached the doorway, Mark laughed at the realization that they would not fit through it. "So much for my courtly gesture. Now I'll have to be rude and precede you." Though Celia knew Emma didn't understand the words, she gurgled with apparent mirth as Mark carried her through the short hallway and opened the door to the storeroom.

"Your surprise, madam." He stood back to let Celia enter the room, Aaron on her heels.

Oh, my! Celia stared in amazement at the transformation of her storage room. The sawing and hammering had told her Mark was building something, but even in her most fanciful moments, she had not expected anything of this magnitude. She had thought he might be constructing a crib for Emma, since he'd mentioned that she would soon outgrow the laundry basket, but this was much more.

"Oh, Mark, it's wonderful!" He had installed five shelves on the long wall. Five beautiful shelves, but that wasn't all. He'd also taken the time to place her canned goods on them. "I can't believe the difference. The room looks twice as big."

Celia had never counted the jars she placed on the floor, but now that they were on the shelves, she saw that she had enough to last the winter. That was a blessing, for it meant less money that she'd need to spend at Frank's store. As she stepped closer, she saw that Mark had even arranged the food by type. What an incredibly thoughtful gesture!

"I won't mistake peaches for pears," she said, hoping her smile told him how grateful she was. "I really don't know how to thank you. The shelves are wonderful, and the organization…I can only imagine how much time that will save me."

Mark's eyes darkened as he nodded. "I'm glad the shelves will save time, but the reason I built them was that I saw you were using the room as a nursery. Pretty soon Emma will start to crawl. That would have been dangerous with all those jars on the floor. She might have wanted to play with them."

Aaron tugged on Mark's pant leg. "I no play with jars."

Celia smiled at the child as she walked closer to the shelves. Thanks to Mark, what had been a jumbled room now looked like a pantry with plenty of room for Aaron and Emma to play. With toys, not canned goods. "You know better," she told Aaron, "because you're a big boy. Emma's still a baby." Running her hand over the edge of a shelf and marveling at how smooth it was, Celia smiled again. "Thank you, Mark. This is the best surprise I've ever had."

He gave her a skeptical look. "Didn't your husband…?" He stopped, as if reluctant to pry into her life.

There was no reason to tell him what her marriage had been like, and yet she felt there was no reason not to. "Josef was a kind man, but he wasn't one for surprises. He would have made shelves for me—not as beautiful as these but serviceable shelves—if I'd asked for them." And that was the difference. Mark had recognized her need and done the work without being asked. It was a huge difference.

* * *

"My arm says it's gonna snow again." Hiram tapped the forearm that was holding his spoon, and a dumpling fell back into his bowl.

It was Mark's second night in Easton, perhaps his last. He ought to be thinking about what was coming next, but instead he found himself reflecting on how much had changed in little more than twenty-four hours. Tonight Hiram greeted him like an old friend; Aaron pouted when he learned he could not sit next to Mark; even Jacob seemed almost friendly. The table was different too. The cloth looked fancier than last night, and the dishes certainly were. Instead of the sturdy white plates she had used before, Celia had set out delicate-looking dishes painted with roses. Though it didn't seem to bother the other men, Mark hated the thought of eating off them. What if he chipped something? His ma had told him that ladies placed a lot of store on fancy dishes. That was why they used them only on special occasions. But today wasn't special.

Hiram looked at his arm again. "I broke it ten years ago. Ever since then, it's been better than that overpriced barometer Frank has in his store."

Mark looked at Frank, wondering if he'd

be offended by the comment. The man hadn't seemed as prickly tonight, but he didn't strike Mark as being one to accept criticism easily.

Fortunately, Frank appeared to take the comment good-naturedly. "My barometer's a sight prettier than your arm."

Letting out a laugh, Hiram nodded. "Cain't argue with that. So, young man," he said, turning to Mark, "what would you think of being stranded here for the winter? It could happen if we have one of our bad spells."

Mark helped himself to another serving of chicken and dumplings as he considered the possibility. One of the reasons he'd spent the day making shelves for Celia was that it kept him from thinking about leaving. Since no one in Easton had heard of Abe Williams, there was no reason to stay, and yet the prospect of remaining was appealing. When he'd started his quest, Mark had made a rule that he wouldn't linger anywhere, but this time there were no new leads, and that meant there was no reason to leave. He might as well stay in Easton until spring. After all, this was the best food he'd had since he left home, and Celia Anderson was by far the most intriguing landlady he'd ever had.

"I think I'd like to stay," Mark told Hiram, "but I need to find a way to pay for my room and board." Though he didn't relish the idea of working underground, if mining was the only way to earn a living in Easton, he'd do it.

Celia looked up from the bread she was buttering, and the smile she gave him made Mark's heart skip a beat. "You're welcome to stay. You know I have plenty of room. As for payment, you won't owe me anything for months after what you did today."

Frank sputtered as he sent Mark an angry glare.

"That was a gift." Even if he hadn't known she was short on money, Mark would not have accepted payment for his work. Like the minor repairs he'd done, he had made the shelves because he wanted to.

"What kind of gift?" Jacob demanded, his gaze moving from Mark to Celia, his tone so belligerent that Aaron, who had been eating contentedly, looked up at his father.

"Jars," Aaron said.

"Not quite. Mark made the most beautiful shelves for my storeroom," Celia explained. "They're so nice that they deserve to be on display somewhere, not relegated to the back of the house, but I have to admit it's nice to have all those jars off the floor."

Frank reached for the tureen of chicken and dumplings. "You know how to make good sturdy shelves?" His voice held a note of surprise.

"I'm a carpenter by trade." Mark wouldn't mention that his real love was carving, because the men who shared Celia's dinner table didn't appear to care about fancy things. They probably hadn't noticed that she had brought out her good china.

Frank chewed thoughtfully before he spoke. "I reckon the folks in Easton could use a carpenter. Business has been so good at the mercantile that I've been thinking about expanding the store into my back room. I'd need counters and shelves if I did that." He pointed his spoon at Mark. "You interested?"

Jacob did not give Mark a chance to answer. "You think you could make a T-O-Y-B-O-X?" He glanced at his son as he spelled the word. "I could use one in oh, about nine weeks."

Christmas. Of course. It would be a gift for Aaron, and if Mark finished it soon enough, others in town might order items for their families.

"I'd be glad to help both of you," Mark said firmly. "All I need is a place to work." Though he'd used Celia's storage room as a workshop, the location had been less than ideal, resulting in extra work to remove sawdust from the jars. He needed a place of his own where he didn't have to worry about the noise and dust bothering others.

Celia nodded slowly, her blue eyes sparkling as if the thought of Easton having a resident carpenter was somehow exciting. It *was* exciting, at least to Mark.

"You can use my smokehouse if the smell won't bother you," she offered. "It's just standing there vacant."

Ten minutes ago, Mark's future had seemed as bleak as a cloudy November day. Now it was filled with promise.

Hiram gave out a chuckle. "'Pears to me Easton's got itself a carpenter."

And Mark had a home, at least for the winter.

It was time to wash dishes. Frank had left; Hiram was upstairs; Mark had taken the lantern out to inspect the smokehouse. Only Jacob seemed reluctant to go home, and that was unusual, for Aaron had fallen asleep on the floor.

When Celia started to rise, Jacob spoke quickly. "Let me help you with the dishes. I know it's time for you to do them."

Celia blinked. Today, it appeared, was a day for surprises. Never before had Jacob volunteered to help her. The reason both he and

Frank paid her for meals was so they could avoid everything connected with supper other than eating it. No shopping, no cooking, no dishes. It seemed wrong to have someone who paid for a meal help with the cleanup.

"There's no need. I'm used to doing dishes alone. Besides…" She stopped, not wanting to offend Jacob with her concerns. Tonight's dishes weren't ordinary dishes. They were her wedding china. She had decided to use them as a way of making what might have been Mark's last supper here a bit more special.

Jacob's smile said he understood her unspoken fear. "I won't break any, if that's what you're worried about. I've learned to do a lot of things in the months since Rachel died."

And so Celia found Jacob standing next to her in her kitchen. She washed and rinsed the dishes she treasured, trying not to scrutinize him as he dried them. Surely it would not be a tragedy if he broke one, and he did seem to be careful. Still, Celia could not relax. As a child, she and her mother had performed the same tasks, talking and laughing as they washed and dried the pots and pans. Tonight, however, sharing the kitchen seemed awkward. Try though she might, Celia could not always avoid touching Jacob's hands when she passed a dish to him. There was nothing remotely romantic about the touches, and yet they disturbed her. Perhaps it was simply that this was the first time a man had helped her with dishes. Or perhaps it was because the man was Jacob. Celia hadn't felt this way when Mark had been in the kitchen with her.

"We work well together." Jacob's words almost made Celia drop a plate back into the soapy water. Either he was simply being polite, or he didn't feel the same awkwardness she did.

"We're a good team," he continued. "It's like horses: you need to be a matched pair."

Team. Horses. Matched. Celia tried not to sigh as she looked at the dishes still to be washed. How much longer would she be stuck here, doing what used to be a pleasant task with a man who was speaking nonsense?

Jacob rubbed the towel over the plate, then set it carefully on the counter. "I'm not one for fancy speeches. Never needed them with Rachel. She understood me."

Celia wondered where this discussion was heading. One thing was certain: she was not like Rachel, for she did not understand Jacob.

She handed him a bowl, but for once he did not begin to dry it. Instead, he looked at her, his expression sober. "What I'm trying to say is, your mourning period's over, and so is mine. Aaron needs a mother. Emma needs a father. I need a wife, and you need a husband. Will you marry me?"

Celia bit back a nervous laugh. This wasn't the way it happened in storybooks. In novels, there was moonlight and roses. The woman was dressed in a beautiful gown, and the man bent one knee. Here she was, wearing an apron over her weekday dress, her hands stuck in a bucket of soapy water while a man who still held one of her china bowls in his hands proposed marriage. You'd never find this scene in a fairy tale. No reader would believe it.

Celia reached for a towel and dried her hands. Somehow she had to get out of this predicament without hurting a good man. Turning to Jacob, she took the bowl from his hand and placed it on the counter. At least her china was safe, and if she was careful, she would not bruise Jacob's pride. "I don't know what to say." Bertha had been right when she'd claimed that Jacob was courting Celia. If she'd listened to her friend, Celia would have been more prepared. Now all she could think of saying was a blunt "No, never," but that would be cruel, and Jacob didn't deserve that.

Why had he chosen tonight? Other than his occasional comments about Emma needing a father, he had never hinted that he considered Celia anything other than a source of supper and care for his son. Was he concerned by Mark's staying for the winter? Whatever the reason, Jacob was standing less than a yard away from her, waiting for her answer.

Celia took a deep breath as she tried to remember the words the heroines of her favorite novels had used to refuse unwanted suitors. "I'm honored by your proposal," she said, "but I'm not yet ready to marry again." That was the truth, albeit only part of the truth.

Though she had feared Jacob might be dismayed, he nodded, as if he'd expected her refusal. "I can wait. Fact is, I've been thinking about a mail-order bride, but I'd rather marry you. Like I said, we're a matched pair."

Of horses! Celia bit back the words that wanted to spill from her mouth. "I'm sorry, Jacob. I'm not ready, and I don't know when I will be." *Or if.*

Her reluctance didn't seem to bother him. "I'll wait until the first of the year before I advertise for a bride. You can give me your answer on New Year's Day."

That answer would be the same as today's. She wouldn't—she couldn't—marry Jacob. But then he walked into the parlor and picked up Aaron. As he smiled at his drowsy son,

Celia's heart began to melt. There might not be a romantic bone in Jacob's body, but he was a good father. Even if he was wrong about her needing a husband, Jacob was right when he said that Aaron needed a mother and Emma needed a father. Oh, why was this so complicated?

Chapter Four

November had never been his favorite month. In most of the places he'd spent it, everything was gray and bleak, the trees bare, the grass brittle and turning brown. It was, to Mark's way of thinking, a peculiar time to consider giving thanks, and yet President Lincoln had chosen this month for national thanksgiving. Mark had joined in the celebrations wherever he had happened to be, but always in the past, he had felt as if he were an outsider. This year was different. This year he was looking forward to the holiday, and—to his surprise—he was filled with gratitude.

Perhaps it was because Easton was prettier than most towns, even now. Since the majority of its trees were conifers, there were few bare branches to remind him that summer had passed, and the sky—far from being leaden gray—was a deep blue that provided a striking contrast to the dark green trees. Even the grass, now dormant and golden, seemed part of a vibrant landscape when it was not covered with snow.

But the natural beauty was only part of the reason for Mark's uncharacteristic cheerfulness. He was enjoying both his new workshop and his first two carpentry jobs. Though the converted smokehouse would probably always smell of smoke and curing meat, the odor was no longer overwhelming, and the tight construction made it ideal for his purposes. He'd hung lanterns from the rafters and along the walls, giving him the light he needed, and had installed a low shelf to hold his tools. It was a simple shop, far different from the one he'd had in Ohio, and yet it met his needs. For the first time in more than two years, his tools were readily accessible, his clamps and saws cleaned and ready for use. It had not been a hardship, working out of a bag, but this was better. Much better.

The work itself was more challenging than the simple repairs that had paid for his food and lodging while he searched for his father. Mark had started on the addition to Frank's store and had new shelves in place. Now, while he waited for the delivery of the hardwood he'd ordered for the cabinets, he had begun Aaron's Christmas gift.

"Good afternoon, Mr. Williams." Mark turned at the sound of the man's voice. "Is your shop open for customers?"

Mark nodded. He wasn't surprised to see Reverend Pearson, for the minister was probably checking on Celia, assuring himself that Mark was not threatening her happiness in any way, but he was surprised by the man's use of the word *customers*. He hadn't expected any additional business until he'd finished either the toy box or the work for Frank.

"The shop sure is open for customers. I can't have too many of them."

The parson took a few steps inside, looking at the changes Mark had made to the humble structure, eventually stopping next to the worktable. A smile crossed his face at the sight of the nearly finished toy box. "Is this the box you're making for Jacob? Mind if I take a closer look?" The tall thin man bent down and touched the joint that Mark had just finished. "That's mighty fine construction."

There was no doubting the man's sincerity, and the simple praise warmed Mark's heart. He wasn't certain whether Jacob would recognize the effort he'd put into the box, but it was gratifying to have someone appreciate his craftsmanship.

"Thank you. You probably know those are dovetail joints. They're more work than simple butted ends, but they're sturdier—what a boy needs." Jacob hadn't specified anything more than a medium-sized wooden box with a lid.

"You know little boys." A hint of humor colored the minister's words.

"I was one myself. I remember there's a lot of rough and tumble in boys' play."

"There'll be dings and dents in the box before New Year's."

Mark gave his potential customer a conspiratorial smile. "I see your memories of childhood are similar to mine." By the time he'd outgrown it, Mark's toy box had had rounded corners and several large chips. He hoped this box would have a similar fate, for it would mean it was being used.

Reverend Pearson ran his hands along the side of the box again. "This will make a fine gift. Ever since Jacob told me you were making this, I've been thinking about gifts. I'd like to give Bertha a blanket chest. About the same size and construction. She won't dent it, of course, but I want one that will last." His eyes narrowed, and he paused, as if uncertain of Mark's reaction to whatever he was going to say next. "The thing is, it seems like it ought to be fancier. A grown woman's needs are different from a little boy's."

"You're right. Ladies like folderol." Look at Celia and her roses. They were everywhere. It wasn't just the parlor. The cabinet in the dining room displayed her china with all its painted roses, and the curtains in the kitchen had a rose print on them. Mark had thought the storage room had escaped until he noticed that one of the blankets lining Emma's makeshift bassinette had rosebuds embroidered around the edge. Yes, indeed. Ladies liked fancy things.

"I could do some carving on the lid— maybe put your wife's initials there." When the minister nodded his approval but seemed to seek something more, Mark added, "I could bead the edges too, if you like. Here's what beading looks like." He pulled a sample from the shelf. Though he'd carried it all the way from Ohio, this was the first time he'd had a customer who might be interested. "What do you think?"

Reverend Pearson nodded again, this time vigorously. "I like it. If you think of anything else, just add it to the box. I trust your judgment. To my way of thinking, the chest can't be too pretty for my wife." He touched the toy box again. "I forgot to ask. Can you have it ready for Christmas?"

"Of course. I had another thought, though. Do you want the chest lined with cedar? It's a bit more work and expense, but my ma used to claim cedar kept the moths away. That might be handy if Mrs. Pearson is storing blankets in it."

"Good idea. My ma used to say the same thing. Now, how much is this going to set me back?"

When Mark gave him a price, the minister stared at him for a long moment, as if he were assessing more than the price. When he spoke, his words were not what Mark expected. Instead of a protest, the parson said, "That seems fair enough. I figured I'd have to pay more."

Mark shrugged. In another time and place, he might have asked for more. "My needs are simple enough. I don't have to overcharge anyone."

Reverend Pearson held out his hand to seal the deal with a shake. "You're a man of integrity. The town can use folks like you." He stared into the distance for a moment before turning back to Mark. "I might not have told you this three weeks ago, but I'm sorry your pa isn't here. If you decide to give up your search, I hope you'll stay in Easton. We can use a permanent carpentry shop, and you'd get customers from Cedarville too."

Mark tried not to let his surprise show. This was a far cry from the suggestion that he find a room in the nearby town. Surely it wasn't because Mark knew how to construct dovetail joints and that he didn't gouge his customers. More likely Reverend Pearson realized that he wasn't a threat to Celia.

"Thank you, Reverend. I appreciate your confidence. The fact is, though, I won't rest well until I find my father, so come spring, I'll be gone."

"What if you don't find him?"

It was a question Mark had asked himself on the darkest of nights. He gave the minister the same answer he gave himself. "I will. Pa has to be somewhere. After that, who knows? I might decide to settle down."

Reverend Pearson nodded. "Easton's a good place for that." He paused for a second then said, "One other thing. I wouldn't be doing my job if I didn't tell you that I hope you'll attend church while you're here. You'd be welcome."

The warmth that the minister's approval had engendered was replaced by a chill. "You're wrong there, Reverend. God wouldn't welcome me in his house." Mark knew that as surely as he knew that the sun would set in a few hours. His mother had claimed that God was loving and caring. She was wrong. If God had cared about Mark and Ma, he wouldn't have let his father desert them.

"Crown me." Celia looked at the checkerboard. One more play and she'd have Mark's last checker. Although she had come close on previous evenings, this was the first time she would be the winner. She knew she ought to feel a sense of elation at the victory, for Mark was a formidable opponent, fierce in his determination to master the checkerboard, but what felt even better than besting him at a game was the camaraderie they had established over the past few weeks.

The one good thing about being a widow was that Celia had fewer restrictions than she would have as a single woman, and no one looked askance at her being unchaperoned once Hiram headed upstairs. It had become a nightly occurrence for Celia and Mark to spend the quiet time after supper together. Some evenings they would play checkers. Other nights they'd simply talk. The common element was that each evening Celia felt as if she was one step closer to understanding the man who boarded with her.

He was more complex than anyone she'd ever met. On the surface, he appeared to be a talented carpenter with a smile for everyone, a savvy businessman who knew how to make each customer feel as if his order was the most important one he had ever received, but despite the outward bonhomie, Celia sensed hidden depths to Mark. At unguarded moments, she would see a sadness in his eyes, and she wondered if it was related to his father. Other times she was certain he was battling anger, and she questioned its cause.

She looked at the man who occupied so many of her thoughts. After he crowned her checker, he studied the board, furrows forming between his eyes. At last he looked up and raised his hands in surrender.

"I give up," he said with a grin. "You told me tonight was going to be your night, and you were right. You beat me fair and square." He lowered his arms and leaned back in his chair, the picture of a man at ease. "You're a remarkable woman, Celia Anderson, and you learn quicker than anyone I've met. Is there anything you can't do?"

Celia felt a flush rise to her cheeks. She wasn't accustomed to praise, especially not from a man. "There are lots of things I can't do. I can't build shelves like yours."

Mark shook his head as he gathered the checkers and poured them into the drawstring bag. "I'll bet you could if you had a little training. It seems to me you can do just about anything. Take dinner as an example. My ma was a good cook, but that beef stew tonight was the best I've ever tasted."

Celia tried to suppress a smile as she wondered whether or not to tell him the truth. "I'm not surprised it didn't taste like your mother's stew. It was venison."

Mark started to chuckle. "That's it. That's the proof I needed. Now you'll never convince me there's something you can't do. The last time I ate venison, I almost spit it out, but this was delicious."

Celia's flush deepened. Mark acted as if preparing a simple stew was a heroic feat. "The venison you ate might have been old, or maybe it wasn't seasoned properly."

"Once again you're proving my point. You know which herbs to use. So, tell me, Celia, is there anything you can't do?"

"Well, there is one very important thing. It seems as if everyone in town has made it their mission to remind me that I can't be a father to Emma." Jacob hadn't said anything more since the night he'd proposed marriage, but Frank had begun talking about how difficult it must be to raise a child alone and how lonely the life of a bachelor was. Though he hadn't voiced the words, the looks he'd given her had made Celia suspect he thought the solution to both of those problems was marriage.

Mark nodded slowly, and the sadness that she'd seen before shone from his eyes. "They're not wrong," he told her. "Growing up, I always felt there was a huge void in my life because I didn't have a father. I don't tell most folks the story, but I guess there's no harm in your knowing." Mark clenched his fists, releasing them slowly as he said, "Ma told me my father died when I was a baby. I didn't know the truth—that he had left us but was still alive—until her death. That's when I discovered the letters he'd sent. It seems he sent money too. Ma wouldn't say much about him. Then when I found the letters, I realized that what she did say was mostly lies." Mark stared at the far wall for a moment. "I guess it doesn't matter. Whether he was dead or alive, he wasn't there while I was growing up."

Celia gripped her chair arms as she tried to imagine the pain Mark had endured. It was no wonder she had seen both sorrow and anger in his expression. Mark had lost more than his father; he'd lost his faith in his mother, for it was obvious he had felt betrayed by both his father's abandonment and his mother's lies.

"I'm so sorry." The words weren't enough, but she wanted him to know that her heart ached for him.

"It's over now." Mark shrugged as if he believed that. Celia did not.

"I was more fortunate than you. I had two loving parents and a very happy childhood."

"Will you tell me about it?" The expression in Mark's eyes told Celia he wanted to shift the attention from himself.

Celia shrugged. "There's not much to tell. We lived in Sweden until twelve years ago. Then some men in our town convinced Papa that there were fortunes to be made in America." Celia shook her head, remembering how strange Wyoming Territory had seemed after the lush farmlands of her first home. "Papa never made a fortune, but even when times were hard, I didn't feel poor, because I knew he and Mama loved me."

Mark nodded as if he understood. She wondered if he did, if his mother had lavished love on him. "Everything changed when my parents died and left me a small inheritance. I didn't know what to do. I didn't want the money. I wanted them."

Once again Mark nodded, and this time

Celia knew he understood. He would have given anything to have his father with him as he was growing up. "Did you use your inheritance?" he asked.

It was Celia's turn to nod. "Josef didn't want to spend it, but after he was gone, I used it to buy this house. It may sound silly, but I feel closer to my parents here than I did in the little house where we used to live."

Celia dropped her gaze to her lap, remembering the emptiness she'd felt after her parents' deaths.

Mark waited until she was looking at him before he spoke. "How long ago did they die?"

"Five years. It was soon after Josef and I married. We'd been living with them, so we just stayed on in that house."

"And you have no brothers or sisters?"

Celia shook her head. "No aunts and uncles, either. Both of my parents were only children. So were Josef's."

Mark's eyes darkened, and this time Celia suspected the sorrow she saw was directed at her. "So you're alone now. Most women would consider that a reason to remarry."

It was an argument Bertha had used on numerous occasions, the sequel to the "Emma needs a father" speech. Like Bertha, Mark meant well. Celia was certain of that, but she was also certain that the seemingly obvious solution was not the best one for her. She forced a laugh. "I guess I'm not most women." Knowing what was coming next, she continued, "I suppose you think I ought to marry Jacob or Frank."

To her surprise, Mark flinched as if she'd hurled a heavy object at him. He was silent for a moment before he said slowly, "They're good men. You never can be sure what's inside a man's heart, but they both look like they'd be good fathers for Emma."

"That's not enough." The words were out of Celia's mouth before she realized what she was saying. She hadn't told anyone, not even Bertha, why she was in no hurry to remarry. It wasn't Bertha's business, she had reasoned, and it certainly wasn't Mark's. And yet, somehow it seemed important that he understood.

"There's not just Emma to consider. There's me too." Celia leaned forward, as if bridging the distance between them would help Mark realize how vital this was to her. "My parents and Josef's arranged our marriage. That's the way it was done in the Old Country, and my parents were like many other immigrants. They clung to the old traditions. No one thought it odd that Josef and I barely knew each other before we were married. That was simply the way it was done. Parents decided who their children should wed."

When Mark said nothing, Celia continued. "Josef was a good man, and I grew to love him, but ours wasn't the kind of marriage I dreamt about, and it certainly wasn't the kind I read about."

A raised eyebrow telegraphed Mark's feelings. "Are you talking about novels? They're not real."

"No, they're not." Celia thought of her less-than-fairy-tale proposal from Jacob. "The stories may not be real, but the love they portray is. I've seen it. I want a husband who looks at me the way Reverend Pearson looks at Bertha. I want a man who will love me for myself, not for my cooking or because I would be a mother to his son or even because he's lonely." Celia closed her eyes for a second before she said, "I want a man who will give me roses for Christmas."

When she opened her eyes, Mark was staring at her, his expression inscrutable. "That's a pretty tall order. Roses don't grow in December, leastwise not in Wyoming Territory."

Was he laughing at her? Celia couldn't believe she'd told him her dearest wish. It sounded so silly when she said it out loud. At night, when she'd lain awake, thinking of her future and Emma's, it had seemed romantic—a man who would indulge her love for the sweetest of flowers, a man who would put beauty and Celia's happiness before practicality. But now it just seemed foolish.

Forcing a laugh to cover her embarrassment, Celia gave Mark a wry smile. "Then I guess I won't marry again."

Chapter Five

"You fixin' to take someone to the Thanksgivin' dinner?"

Mark looked up from the cabinet edge he was scribing. Though Frank might not notice a gap of a fraction of an inch, Mark was determined that the cabinet would fit flush to the wall, and that required concentration. Unfortunately, it was difficult to concentrate when Daniel kept interrupting. The boy who had directed Mark to Celia's boardinghouse the day he'd arrived in Easton seemed determined to help him, although that help had actually delayed Mark's progress.

"Nope." Mark doubted his answer would discourage Daniel. Nothing seemed to discourage him, not even his obvious lack of skill with a saw and hammer. One of the disadvantages of this final stage of Frank's store expansion was that it required Mark to work on-site, and that meant constant interruptions from Daniel. Whenever there was a lull between customers, he hurried to the back room to assist Mark.

Daniel's eyes widened in surprise—or perhaps it was disappointment. Since Mark had been working in the mercantile, Daniel had treated him like some kind of hero. The boy's claim that he wanted to be a carpenter like Mark had elicited a guffaw from Frank. Daniel, the store owner claimed, changed his plans along with the bathwater each Saturday night, and Mark should pay him no mind. But Mark, who knew how devastating discouraging words could be, didn't want to destroy Daniel's ambition, and so he let him carry in pieces of wood and watch while Mark assembled them. The work would have taken less time if he'd been alone, and he wouldn't have had the distraction of Daniel's chatter, but those were prices Mark was willing to pay.

"How come not? Thanksgiving's more fun if you go with someone special." Daniel leaned against the wall, his eyes narrowing as he considered either the way Mark was carefully planing the cabinet edge or his refusal to escort one of Easton's eligible young women to the celebration.

For his part, Mark was startled by the jolt of pleasure he'd felt when Daniel had pronounced the words "someone special." Celia fit that description to a T. He had no doubt that the dinner would be more enjoyable if she were at his side.

"I'm not sure I'm going at all," Mark admitted. While everyone else in Easton was talking about Thanksgiving, his thoughts were focused on Christmas—Christmas roses, to be precise. Ever since Celia had told him she wanted a man to give her roses for Christmas, Mark had thought of little else. More than anything he could remember, he wanted to be the man who made her dream come true, and yet...

"You gotta go." The horrified expression on Daniel's face spoke volumes. "Everybody in Easton will be there, plus all the folks from Cedarville." When Mark didn't respond, Daniel continued. "The food is mighty good."

Since he'd arrived in Easton, Mark had been no stranger to good food. Celia's meals were more than good. Everything she cooked was delicious, making a man want second or even third helpings, and yet when Mark complimented her, he often saw a pained expression flit across her face. Did she think that was all he cared about? Perhaps she did, for he couldn't forget her saying that she wanted a man to value her for herself, not her cooking. It was true that he appreciated her cooking, but his admiration for Celia went far deeper than that.

He ran his hand over the side of the cabinet, checking for splinters and rough spots. The wood was smooth, but not as smooth as Celia's skin. Though he'd never touched her cheek, Mark knew that. All he had to do was look at her to know that her skin was as soft as the petals of those roses she loved so much. He bent his head, not wanting Daniel to view the confusion in his eyes. Mark had seen pretty women before; he'd met kind women before; but none of them had lingered in his memory the way Celia did. He couldn't forget her sunny smile or the delicate scent of roses that clung to her. Most of all, he couldn't forget the love that shone from her eyes when she looked at Emma. That was his problem.

Mark frowned as he slid the cabinet into place. The townspeople were right. Emma needed a father. More than that, she *deserved* a father. That sweet little girl deserved a man who'd cherish her as much as her mother did, who'd teach her the things only a father could, and who'd protect her from life's dangers. The problem was, Mark didn't know the first thing about being a father, and he sure as the sun set early in November wasn't going to risk a child's future happiness on the chance that he could learn. What if he was as inept at being a father as Daniel was at hammering a nail?

"You really oughta go. Food's even better than Christmas." Daniel appeared to be waiting for Mark's response.

"I imagine it is," he said, grateful for the excuse to think of something—anything—other than Celia and Emma, "but I reckon I'll be working that day. I need to be sure everything will be ready for Christmas." Mark had been surprised by the number of orders he'd received. Although a few women had come to his shop, the majority of his customers had been men who claimed that Reverend Pearson had told them about his work. In addition to boxes designed to hold jewelry, he had commissions for plate racks, small tables, even a pair of bookends for the schoolteacher. The parson hadn't been exaggerating when he claimed that Easton could use a carpenter.

When he'd finished installing the cabinet, Mark returned to his workshop and studied the blanket chest he was making for the minister's wife. The box itself was finished, the scent of the cedar lining battling with the smokehouse walls for supremacy. All that remained was the lid. Mark had drawn a design of Mrs. Pearson's initials and was ready to carve it into the top, but, even though he'd chosen elaborately curling letters, he needed something more. Roses for Christmas. The thought circled through his head, reminding him once again of Celia and the night she'd told him why she wouldn't remarry. Mark studied his drawing. No doubt about it, the chest would be beautiful if he surrounded Bertha Charlotta Pearson's initials with a wreath of roses, but he wouldn't. Perhaps he would use lilies. Roses were for Celia…and Emma.

As he started sketching a circlet of lilies, Mark envisioned Emma in fifteen years. She'd be a beauty, just like her mother, and Celia would find herself having to fend off her daughter's suitors. He could picture the pimply faced boys lined up to see Emma, while Celia stood guard like that big old shepherd dog Ma had put near the henhouse. That sure would be something to see. But Mark wouldn't be here.

She was content. The thought washed over her like the pictures she had seen of ocean waves breaking over a rock, startling her with its intensity. Here she was, sitting in her storage room, rocking Emma and listening to

Aaron sing silly songs while she waited for the bread to bake. It was an ordinary afternoon, and yet Celia felt more content than she could ever remember. Perhaps it was foolish, for the future remained uncertain. If she didn't get at least one more boarder after Mark left, she wasn't confident she would be able to keep the house. Perhaps she ought to worry about that, but today she couldn't. At least for this afternoon, she was happy.

Emma was healthy. Just last week, she'd smiled at Celia and jabbered something that sounded like Mama, making Celia's heart overflow with happiness. Aaron made her laugh with his nonsensical ditties, and then there was Mark. Celia had never met a man like him. It wasn't simply that he was more handsome than anyone in Easton, although she had heard the single women discussing that particular fact in great detail when they gathered after church services. It wasn't simply that she found his conversation stimulating or that she enjoyed the challenge of trying to beat him at checkers. What drew Celia to the undeniably handsome man who rented her best room was his thoughtfulness. Mark was unfailingly kind, but more than that, he anticipated her needs almost before she was aware of them. There were times when she felt as if they were two halves of the same whole.

And then she would catch a flash of his anger. Though he tried to hide it, it would emerge at unpredictable times. Sometimes it was the mention of a child that brought it out, and Celia knew he was remembering his childhood without a father. Sometimes it was a casual reference to church or to God. He said little, merely shaking his head when Celia asked if he wanted to accompany her to Sunday services, and Celia would not press him.

Frank had no such reservations. "You a heathen?" he had asked at supper last night.

Mark took a sip of water before he responded. "What makes you think that?"

"I haven't seen you at church."

Mark sighed, and Celia sensed his reluctance to say anything more. Whatever his problem was with God, it was between him and God. Frank had no right to interfere. "I used to go to church," Mark said. "Every week, in fact. But I wouldn't be welcome there anymore."

"Folks are friendly here. They welcome most everyone." Jacob entered the conversation.

"It's not the townspeople I'm worried

about," Mark countered. Though he said nothing more, Celia had felt tears well in her eyes.

Emma stirred, bringing Celia back to the present. How selfish she was, sitting here, counting her blessings, when Mark was in pain. He might express it as anger, but she had seen the anguish in his eyes. He was troubled, and there was nothing she could do for him other than pray. Preaching didn't work. Celia knew that. When she'd been angry with God after Josef was killed, both Bertha and Reverend Pearson had counseled her to put aside her anger. It wasn't that simple.

No matter how much she cared for him, and Celia would not deny that she had more than friendly feelings for Mark, she could not change what was inside his heart. But, oh, how she wished she could help him.

"Celia?"

She blinked, startled by the sound of Frank's voice. Was she late? A quick look at her watch confirmed that it was only three o'clock, two and a half hours before supper would be served. Frank never came this early.

"We're in the storage room," she called out, rising and laying Emma in her basket. Apparently annoyed at being disturbed, Emma started to fuss.

"I fix, Mrs. Celia." Aaron put his arms

around Emma and began to croon to her. To Celia's amazement, the ploy worked.

"Thank you, Aaron." Celia turned toward Frank, who stood in the doorway, a brown paper-wrapped box in his hands. "Is something wrong?" Though Frank sometimes worked in the back room and let Daniel wait on customers, he never left the store before closing time.

He shook his head. "I just wanted a chance to see you alone." Frowning slightly, Frank looked down at Aaron, as if the young boy's presence were a nuisance.

"Oh, well…" Celia knew Aaron could be counted on to play by himself for a few minutes. "I suppose we could go into the parlor." With the doors open, she would be able to hear Emma if she fussed. "I have bread baking, and when it comes out, I need to put tonight's cobbler into the oven."

Frank shifted the box from one hand to the other, then nodded. "The parlor would be nice."

When they were seated in the matching chairs on either side of the small table where she and Mark played checkers, Frank held out the package. "I brought you a token of my affection."

Affection. That was what Celia felt for Aaron. It was not something she sought from this man. Trying not to frown, she kept her voice even as she said, "Thank you, but that wasn't necessary." She wouldn't insult Frank by telling him that she didn't want his affection. There had to be another, more subtle way, to make him understand that their relationship was purely business. "You pay me fairly for the meals you take here."

He shook his head, and his eyes darkened momentarily when she did not accept the proffered package. "This has nothing to do with meals. It's for you."

Short of being rude, there was no way to refuse the gift, and Mama had taught Celia that a lady was never rude. She managed a small smile as she reached for the box, but her smile broadened when she slid the twine from the package and opened the wrapping. Though Frank might call the gift a token of his affection, the contents were not personal. Instead of the flowers, books, and candy that Mama had claimed were traditional courting gifts, Frank had brought her a tin of oysters.

"Thank you, Frank." Not just for the exotic food but also for the fact that they could not be construed as part of a courtship ritual. According to Mama, no man would give a woman he favored something that required her to work. Courtship was a time to pamper a lady, not remind her of housewifely tasks. "I've never eaten oysters, but I understand they're delicious." Oysters were one of the most costly food items at Frank's store, far too expensive for Celia's limited budget.

He grinned, as if her earlier reluctance were forgotten. "I got a new shipment today and figured you'd like them. You're a mighty fine cook, Celia. You could turn them into oyster stew or pudding."

Perhaps Frank was giving her a not-so-subtle hint that he'd like more variety in his meals. Celia hoped that was the reason for his visit, although the gleam in his eye suggested otherwise. "It's kind of you to say that. And now…"

When she started to rise, Frank held out a hand to stop her. "I've got one more thing to ask. I was hoping you'd let me escort you to the Thanksgiving dinner."

Celia took a deep breath, inhaling the aroma of cloves that seemed to be his trademark scent. Bertha had been right. Frank was interested in having Celia cook for him permanently. "Thank you, but—"

Before she could complete her sentence, he frowned. "I waited until your year of mourning was over. I don't mind telling you it was hard to wait. You're a mighty pretty woman. Any man would be proud to have you on his arm."

At least he hadn't told her they were matched like horses. Celia knew she ought to be grateful for that, even though his words made her feel like a possession, not a woman. "Be kind," Mama had always said. Celia would be kind, but she would also be firm. "I appreciate your compliments, Frank, but I don't want to lead you on. I'm not ready for anything other than friendship. Emma and I will go to the dinner as part of a group." Unlike Jacob, Frank had said nothing about Emma, and that chafed. Surely he must realize that Emma was the most important part of Celia's life and that she wouldn't do anything that wasn't good for her daughter.

"I see." Frank's eyes narrowed. "Will that group include Mark?"

She wouldn't lie. "Probably. I expect Hiram will be with us too. Reverend and Mrs. Pearson have asked us to sit with them."

"I know he's younger than me." It appeared that Frank had dismissed her statements about Hiram and the Pearsons, for Mark was the only man in the group younger than him. "He's practically a vagabond. He's going to leave, and then you'll be alone."

Celia nodded. As angry as Frank was, he

spoke nothing but the truth. "Mark's a boarder. Of course he'll leave. They all do."

She wouldn't add the thought that sometimes kept her awake at night: it would be different when Mark left. That void would not be easily filled. Perhaps it never would be.

Mark took a deep breath as he poised his chisel over the lid of the blanket chest, preparing to take the first cut. Whether the design was simple or intricate, there was always a rush of excitement when he reached this stage. He smiled at the thought of Bertha Pearson's pleasure on Christmas morning when she saw her blanket chest. The cedar lining made it practical. The lily-bordered monogram would make it special.

"Mark! Mark! Help me!"

As the shout startled him, Mark's chisel slipped from his hand, gouging the wood. Sparing little more than a glance for the now-wrecked lid, he wheeled around. He'd worry about Mrs. Pearson's gift later. Right now what was important was that Celia needed him. The panic in her voice told him this was no trivial matter. Had she scalded herself? Had a knife slipped? As his mind conjured horrible images, Mark sprinted toward the house and flung the door open.

Celia stood in the center of the hallway, clutching Emma to her.

From the corner of his eye, Mark saw Aaron sitting on the floor, his eyes wide with worry. "Feel her head," Celia said. "Emma's burning with fever. She was fine when she woke this morning, and then the next thing I knew, she was like this."

Mark touched the baby's forehead. Celia hadn't exaggerated. Emma's face was unnaturally hot. He had heard that some infants were prone to high fevers, and the number of tiny graves in most cemeteries was silent witness to just how dangerous those fevers could be.

"What should I do?" Emotion choked Celia's voice. "I tried cool compresses, but they didn't help."

The only remedy Mark knew was immersing the patient in a cold bath, but that was risky. While a bath would sometimes break the fever, it could also cause more problems. "I'll fetch Doc." If the God Celia was so fond of quoting was truly a loving God, the doctor would be in town today, and he'd know how to help her daughter.

Emma started to wail, balling her tiny hands and beating them against her forehead. Mark's heart sank. The child must be in intense pain to do that. There was no time to waste. If he were certain that Doc was in his office, Mark would have taken Emma there, but he didn't want to expose her to the frigid outside air unnecessarily. Her breathing was already shallow and rapid.

"Your coat," Celia cried as Mark headed for the door.

He shook his head. There wasn't time to worry about that. All that mattered was getting help for Emma. Quickly. He raced down the street, ignoring the curious looks of two matrons who were strolling toward the mercantile. The physician's office was in the building on the far side of the church.

"You've got to come," Mark shouted as he flung open the door. Fortunately the doctor was seated behind his desk in the front room, and there appeared to be no other patients. "Emma's sick. A fever."

Though he rose, Doc appeared in no hurry. He gave Mark a quizzical look. "You're Miz Anderson's new boarder." Methodically, he buttoned his coat before reaching for his medical bag and looking around the room as if to assure himself that he needed nothing more. When he seemed satisfied that he would not require any of the multicolored bottles that filled a glass-fronted cabinet, the doctor nodded. "Heard about you. Quick thinking on your part. Croup," he added in explanation.

Mark had heard stories about the doctor's peculiar way of speaking. He didn't care that the man would never be an orator. Doc didn't have to say a word, so long as he cured whatever was causing Emma's fever. But first he had to get to the boardinghouse. They were outside now, and though the doctor was walking briskly, Mark couldn't contain his impatience. "Hurry," he said, increasing his own stride to just under a run. "She's got a fever."

The doctor nodded but kept his own pace steady. "Not uncommon. New mothers panic."

Mark wouldn't accept that explanation. "This is Celia we're talking about. She's not one to panic." Although Mark had to admit that her agitation had been only one step shy of it.

"Maybe. Maybe not."

And the doctor said not another word until they reached the boardinghouse. When they entered the house, they found Celia still standing in the back hallway, her face white with fear as she looked down at Emma. The only difference Mark could see was that Aaron was now clinging to Celia's skirts.

"Let me have her." The doctor held out his arms. Striding into the kitchen, he looked around, then placed Emma on the table. As he began to undress her, the baby started to cry, and Celia took a step toward her daughter.

"No." The doctor's command was brusque. He appeared to be examining each of the flailing limbs as he uncovered them, his expression serious.

Celia's lips started to tremble, and Mark wondered if she would be the next to cry. She might brush him aside, but he had to do something. Wrapping his arm around Celia's shoulders, he drew her close to him. "Emma will be all right," he said softly, trying to reassure her. "Doc's here."

The doctor rummaged in his medical bag for a moment, withdrawing a stethoscope and an instrument Mark had seen other physicians poke into a patient's ears. He'd never learned the name for that.

"It's just routine," Mark whispered as Doc plugged his stethoscope into his ears and listened to Emma's breathing. Though he wanted to reassure Celia, even Mark knew that Emma's breathing wasn't normal. He tightened his arm, bringing Celia closer to him, hoping she would accept the comfort he offered. Her trembling seemed to have lessened, but the fact that she paid no attention to the anxious toddler at her side told Mark that Celia was still caught in the grip of her fears.

He extended his free arm and placed his hand on Aaron's head. "You're a big boy," he said. "Big boys don't cry."

Aaron raised his tearstained face and nodded. "I big."

It seemed as if the physician poked and prodded Emma for an eternity, but Mark knew it was only a minute or two. At last, Doc looked up.

"Just what I thought. Common aftereffect of croup."

Though the doctor didn't sound concerned, Mark wished he'd say something more. "Will Emma be all right?"

"Of course." Doc nodded as he slid his instruments back into his bag. "Fever should break in a few hours. Cold compresses help. Takes awhile, though."

Celia slumped ever so slightly, and Mark knew it was with relief. "Your instincts were right," he said as he released her. "The compresses were helping." She gave him a watery smile before crossing the short distance to her daughter and beginning to dress her.

"Thank you, Doctor. I feel better now." Celia's voice sounded better too. The strain was gone, as was the threat of tears.

A brusque nod was the doctor's only response. While Celia cradled her daughter and Aaron chattered about the doctor's bag and his stethoscope, Mark walked to the door with the physician.

"Are you certain she'll be all right?"

Doc raised an eyebrow, making Mark wonder if he were annoyed that someone dared to question his judgment. "As sure as anyone can be. Normal for Miz Anderson to worry. Almost lost her daughter before. This is not serious."

"Thank you." As Mark extended his hand to shake the doctor's, Aaron skittered to a stop next to him.

The doctor gave Mark's hand a brief shake, then fixed another quizzical look on him. "You remind me of someone. Been nagging at me since you stormed into the office." He stared at Mark's face, as if memorizing his features. "Problem is, can't remember who."

Chapter Six

"You'll be all right, sweetie," Celia said as she wrung out the cloth and placed the cold compress on her daughter's head. She'd repeated the action dozens of times since the doctor had left. Each time she removed the compress, Celia felt Emma's head, and each time she frowned, for there appeared to be no change. This time was different. It might be nothing more than her imagination, but it seemed as if Emma was a bit cooler. Celia shivered. Although her daughter might be burning with fever, she was so cold that her teeth chattered. Fear did that to a person. She'd been shivering ever since she'd realized that her precious child was ill.

"The doctor says this helps," she crooned as Emma protested having her forehead covered with a cold cloth. He'd also said that it would take awhile, and he'd been right, for it was the middle of the night and the fever had yet to subside. Celia watched as her daughter tried to brush the compress away. Perhaps it wasn't her imagination that Emma was cooler, for this was the first time she'd done more than lie there, her passivity a symptom that all was not well. Perhaps the fever was breaking, and they'd both be able to sleep.

Celia removed the cloth from Emma's head, placing her hand on her daughter's temples. It wasn't her imagination. The fever was gone. "Thank you, Lord." She sank to her knees and bowed her head. "Thank you for healing Emma and for sending Mark."

Mark had been a gift. While she had been practically paralyzed with fear, his presence had comforted her as much as—perhaps even more than—the doctor's diagnosis. When he had stood next to her, his arm wrapped around her shoulders, Celia had felt as if they were a family: she, Mark, and Emma. Mark had shared the burden of her fears, and for those moments when only a heartbeat had separated them, she had not been alone. She knew it wouldn't happen again, and yet it had felt so good that Celia wished there were some way to capture those feelings, saving them for the years that stretched out in front of her.

* * *

Mark smiled as he carved another lily onto the blanket chest. It seemed like a small miracle, but dropping his tools onto the lid hadn't destroyed it. When he'd returned to the workshop after Celia had taken Emma to her room, he'd inspected the damage, expecting to have to replace the entire top. Instead, he'd discovered that the chisel had dug into the lid at one of the spots he had planned to remove to create a lily. He wouldn't have to make another top, and he wouldn't be behind schedule with his Christmas orders. Though that was good news, it couldn't compare to the knowledge that Emma's fever had broken.

Celia had delivered that news at breakfast, and Mark knew he'd grinned like a fool, filled with relief. Emma would be fine, and so would her mother. Though her eyes were rimmed with dark circles, testament to the sleepless night, Celia's smile had been brilliant, and Emma had cooed as if she hadn't frightened both her mother and Mark the previous day. Children were far more resilient than adults.

He positioned the gouge, carefully removing the top layers of wood as he began to carve another leaf. Though he couldn't forget his fear, sweeter memories warmed his heart as he worked on Mrs. Pearson's Christmas gift. It had felt unbelievably good to wrap his arm around Celia's shoulders and draw her close to him.

It wasn't his first time to hold a woman, but it had never felt like that. In the past his thoughts had been of what he could take—a touch, a kiss or two. Yesterday had been different. For the first time, he had sought only to give. He had wanted nothing more than to comfort Celia, to provide the strength she so desperately needed. Surprisingly, when she left the shelter of his arms, Mark realized he'd received far more than he'd given. For, while she'd rested her head against his heart, he had felt as if they belonged together. It was impossible, of course. He knew that, and yet it had felt so good, so right, that he'd found himself dreaming of a life in Easton, a life with a wife and daughter who looked exactly like Celia and Emma.

"Mr. Williams?"

Mark turned, his momentary euphoria shattered by the sound of the physician's voice. Doc Rudinski didn't strike him as a man who was looking for carpentry services, and if his solemn expression was any indication, this was not a social call. That meant...

Mark's heart lurched as he asked, "Is Emma all right?"

To Mark's relief, the physician nodded. "Just saw her. Fever's gone." He looked around the room, his eyes darting from one corner to the next. When most people visited the workshop, their attention was drawn to Mark's projects. Doc seemed to be assuring himself that there was no one else in the building. "You're the reason I came," he said brusquely. "Couldn't sleep for thinkin' about you. Folks told me you're looking for your pa." He frowned, as if blaming Mark for his insomnia. "Knew you reminded me of someone. Finally remembered the hermit. Same eyes and nose." The doctor studied Mark's face for a moment. "Yep. You look like the old hermit."

Mark's breath escaped in a whoosh. He'd known that Doc had been treating a hermit somewhere in the woods the day he had arrived in Easton, the day Emma had been so ill with croup, but Mark had given the recluse no further thought. It seemed he should have.

"My father? You think he could be my father?" Mark took a deep breath, trying to settle his nerves. Though he had had dozens of leads, this was the first time in more than two years that anyone had seen a resemblance. In the past, Mark had been so far behind his father that all anyone remembered was his name and the fact that he was a tall man with gray hair. When Mark had shown them the wedding portrait, most people had shrugged. "Mebbe, mebbe not" was the typical reply. This was different. Doc hadn't seen the picture.

Mark inhaled sawdust and varnish and listened to the sound of his own heartbeat while he waited for the response.

"Could be." Nodding once again, the doctor pulled a piece of paper from his pocket and extended it to Mark. "Made a map. Decision's yours."

When Doc left, Mark stared at the blanket chest, then laid down his chisel. It would be foolhardy to try to carve when his mind was whirling. It seemed almost incredible that his father might be less than ten miles away and that his search might have ended. In the back of his mind, Mark had known it was unlikely that his father was living in a small mining town, but he had had no other leads, and he couldn't—he wouldn't—stop searching until he'd followed every trail, no matter how faint.

On nights when he'd been unable to sleep, he had acknowledged the possibility that he would never find his father, that he might have died or simply disappeared. With those thoughts twisting his gut, sleep was impossible, but when daylight broke, the doubts faded like dew on the tall grasses, and Mark knew that he would continue searching. Someday, somewhere he would find his pa.

Mark sank onto a bench as new fears assailed him. What would he say? He had never been this close to finding his father, and so he had never considered what words to use with the man who'd deserted him and his mother. He closed his eyes, trying to picture the scene. What would happen if he started the conversation by demanding to know why his father had left? Would the man reply, or would he simply turn his back? And if he did respond, would the answer bring Mark peace or would it confirm what he feared, that the man who had fathered him didn't love him?

Clenching his fists in frustration as the questions mounted, Mark rose and walked to the door. Opening it, he let the cold air in as he stared at the back of the boardinghouse and tried to corral his thoughts. The hermit might be his pa, but then again, he might not. If he wasn't, what did that mean? He had no other leads. As a knot formed in his stomach, Mark grabbed his jacket. Maybe some coffee would help clear his mind.

A cup of coffee and Celia. That's what he needed.

Celia turned, startled by the sound of the back door opening. She might not have heard the muted creaking on a normal day, but today was unusually quiet, for when Celia had put Emma in the bassinet for her midmorning nap, Aaron had plopped himself on the floor next to her and was now fast asleep.

The firm footsteps told Celia that her visitor was Mark, and that was unusual. He rarely came into the house between meals, especially with so many Christmas gifts to make. There was only one reason Celia could imagine for Mark's presence: he had hurt himself.

"Could I trouble you for a cup of coffee?"

She started to relax. An injured man would not ask for coffee, and yet something was amiss, for Mark's expression was almost as grim as it had been when he'd felt Emma's forehead and realized how high her fever was.

"Coffee's no trouble," Celia said as she pulled a cup off the shelf. "By now you should know that there's always a pot on the stove. My mother used to say you could always tell when a Swede was home by sniffing the air.

If you smelled coffee, it was fine to come in." She gave an exaggerated sniff, hoping that Mark would laugh, but he did not. Instead, his eyes remained somber, and furrows deepened between them as he took a seat at the table and reached for the cup.

Perhaps she should wait for him to speak, but patience was not one of Celia's virtues. "What's wrong?" she asked.

Mark sipped the dark brew. While he stared at the floor as if counting the bits of sawdust that clung to his boots, Celia's concerns multiplied faster than weeds in June. She'd rarely seen his expression so solemn. Something was definitely wrong.

"You're worrying me." She leaned across the table, trying to close the distance between them. Though she wanted to lay her hand on Mark's in a gesture of friendship and comfort, she would not, for that would be unseemly. A lady never initiated a touch, and so she waited for Mark to respond.

When he met her gaze, Celia almost shuddered. Never before had she seen Mark's gray eyes so filled with pain. He swallowed, then laid the cup on the table. "Doc thinks I look like the old hermit living in the woods."

It took a moment for the significance to

register, but when it did, Celia's heart leapt. "That's wonderful!"

Mark shook his head, and though she had not thought it possible, the anguish on his face deepened. Surely this was what he wanted, to be reunited with his father. That was why he had come to Easton.

He picked up the cup and drained it before he spoke. When he did, his voice was so low Celia had to strain to hear it. "I'm not sure I want to meet him."

She took a deep breath, trying to quiet the butterflies that were beating frantically in her stomach. She could understand nervousness but not the dread that colored Mark's voice. "You've been searching for your father for more than two years," she said as calmly as she could. "Why would you do that if you didn't want to meet him?"

A soft cry came from the storage room, telling Celia her daughter was stirring. If she wakened, Aaron would too. *Please, Lord, let her sleep. Let them both sleep. And show me how to help Mark.* For though he might deny it, Mark needed someone to help him make sense of his feelings. Finding his father had been his quest for so long that Celia could not fathom his ambivalence. All she knew was that he could not stop, not now when he was so close to the answers he sought.

When she heard nothing more than Emma's soft snuffling, Celia knew the first part of her prayer had been answered. She would have a few more minutes without interruptions.

She looked at the man who sat opposite her as she searched for the right words. "It's important, Mark. You need to find out whether this man is your father." He gave no sign that he'd heard her. Celia's lips tightened. There had to be a way to get his attention. Casting aside propriety, she reached across the table and placed her hand on Mark's. It was surprising how different his hand felt from hers. His was firmer, the skin rougher, and of course it was much larger, larger even than Josef's had been. "If you don't go, you'll always wonder about the hermit. You need to know the truth. Don't you remember how Jesus said, 'Ye shall know the truth, and the truth shall make you free'?"

Though she had placed her hand on the back of his, Mark turned his over, pressing his palm to hers as he said, "Perhaps."

Waves of warmth washed over Celia. It had been so long since a man had held her hand, and it felt so good that for a second she forgot why she was sitting here, her hand in Mark's.

And then she remembered. "I don't understand why you're hesitating. I know you're not afraid."

Mark's eyes darkened. "Perhaps I am. The truth is, I'm not sure how I'll feel if the man is my father." His voice roughened with something that sounded like anger or perhaps something stronger: hatred.

"Do you hate him?"

Mark threaded his fingers through hers, his expression pensive as he considered Celia's question. "No," he said at last, "but I am angry. There are times when I'm so filled with anger that I feel as if I'll erupt."

Tightening her grip on his hand, Celia nodded slowly. It was what she had thought. Mark harbored deep anger. The only way he would find peace was to release it. "I can understand that. I'd be hurt and angry if my father had left me." As a parent, she couldn't imagine what would have made Mark's father leave his family. Nothing, absolutely nothing, would tear her away from Emma.

"It's not just my father," Mark admitted. "You've asked me why I won't go to church with you. The reason is I'm angry with God." Mark's lips twisted with anger. "Why did he let my father leave? If he's as powerful as everyone claims, he could have stopped my pa. Why didn't he?"

Celia's heart thudded at the pain she heard in Mark's voice. Though his touch had comforted her yesterday, it appeared that hers was not as powerful. Mark needed more. When she had been angry with God, words had not helped her, but perhaps they would help heal Mark. "I asked the same questions when Josef was killed. We both went to church every Sunday. We loved God. We trusted him. So why didn't God stop the mine cart before it crushed my husband?"

Mark's eyes darkened. "Why didn't he? He must have known about Emma and that she would need a father."

Celia's heart resumed its normal beat as Mark echoed her thoughts. He understood what she had felt. Perhaps after he heard her answer, his anger would begin to subside. "I asked myself the same question. When I stopped being numb, I railed at God, demanding to know why he'd abandoned me."

Mark nodded, and she suspected he was thinking of how his earthly father had abandoned him. But God hadn't abandoned her. She simply hadn't understood his ways.

"It took me awhile, but I learned that God's plans aren't the same as mine. I may never know why Josef was killed, but I've learned to trust God's wisdom." She looked down at her hand clasped in Mark's, wishing it were as simple to open his heart as it had been to place her hand on his. "There's a verse in Romans that says God will make everything work out for our good if we trust him."

Raised eyebrows signaled his skepticism. "Do you believe that?"

"I do." Celia had to make him understand what she had learned. It was so very, very important. "I've seen the proof. As awful as it was that your father left you, something good came from it. If he hadn't left, you wouldn't have come to Easton, and my daughter might not still be alive."

Mark stared into the distance for a moment. "That's one way of looking at it. Another is to say it was pure chance that I arrived when I did." His expression left no doubt which explanation he preferred.

"I don't believe in chance or coincidence. I believe that was part of God's plan for me..." Celia paused before adding softly, "And for you."

Shaking his head, Mark turned back to her. "I'm not sure I'll ever believe that, but it's a nice story."

Celia bit back a sigh. "Think about it. That's

all I ask. Just think about your life and see if you can't find evidence of God's hand in it."

"You sound like Ma. She claimed God loved me, and she was always quoting the Ten Commandments. I guess she forgot the one about bearing false witness." Mark's lips curved in a scornful smile. "Why did she lie to me? Why did she tell me Pa was dead when he wasn't? I spent most of my life wondering why she wouldn't remarry and give me a father."

Mark's voice bristled with anger, but underneath that, Celia heard the pain of a young boy trying to understand why his family wasn't like others. Somehow she had to ease that pain. She remained silent for a moment, choosing her words. "I'm trying to imagine how I would have felt if I were in your mother's position," she said slowly. "I know I would have been angry at first. When Josef died, I wasn't just angry with God. I was also angry with Josef for leaving me. Doesn't that sound silly? It wasn't as if he had a choice, but that didn't stop me from blaming him and being angry. I imagine your mother felt some of that." But anger faded; at least Celia's had. What would Mrs. Williams have felt as the weeks turned into months? Celia took a deep breath, exhaling slowly before she said, "I

might have been ashamed that my husband
had left me and our child. If that was the case,
I wouldn't have wanted anyone to know the
truth. I would have done anything I could to
protect my child from the shame of knowing
his father abandoned us, and so I would have
claimed he was dead."

Celia watched the play of emotions on
Mark's face. Surprise mingled with resigna-
tion. "You could be right."

There had been two parts to Mark's question. "Embarrassment would explain the lie.
As for not giving you a stepfather, it's possible your mother had no desire to remarry."

His eyes widened. "Why not? She could
have used help around the farm, and I sure
could have used a father."

Those were practical reasons, the same kind
of reasons the citizens of Easton gave Celia
when they urged her to find another husband.
But the heart didn't always listen to practicality. "I can think of a few reasons. Your mother
might have loved your father so much that she
couldn't imagine loving anyone else. And if
she was protecting you, which I think she was,
she wouldn't have wanted to go through the
shame of a divorce or having him declared
dead, because either case would have required
her to admit that he'd left you." When Mark

said nothing, Celia continued. "Another possibility is that her marriage was unhappy. If she believed it had been a mistake, she might not have wanted to risk repeating it."

Mark's eyes closed briefly, the tightening of his lips giving Celia the impression that he hadn't considered any of the scenes she'd painted.

"It might have been none of those," she said softly. "Maybe she didn't believe the men who courted her would be good fathers. I can't speak for your mother, but I know that I would rather have Emma grow up without a father than with a bad one."

He sighed, and Celia sensed that she'd touched a sensitive cord.

"There's only one way I'll learn the truth," Mark said at last. "I have to find the hermit." His gaze met hers. Though his brow was no longer furrowed, his expression was intense. "I hope you're right. I hope the truth will set me free."

Chapter Seven

"It's too nice a day to be cooped up indoors." Celia slid Aaron's hands into the mittens, tugging until the cuffs covered his wrists. In just a few minutes, she'd have both children bundled into their winter clothes. While it was true that Emma and Aaron would enjoy the outing, Celia's motives were purely selfish. With Emma ensconced in the high-sided wagon and Aaron trotting alongside it, she hoped she would be able to breathe again. When the door had closed behind Mark this morning, a lump had lodged in her throat, making breathing and swallowing painful. She hoped fresh air would dissolve it.

"Cold." Aaron swung his arms back and forth, seemingly entertained by his frosty breath. Though the day was cold, the clear sky told Celia that the sun would soon warm the air. Aaron would do what he always did when they took an excursion: run as fast as his short legs would permit, then race back, bend over the wagon, and tell Emma everything he'd seen. For her part, Emma would coo at him, occasionally punctuating her gibberish with pumps of her mittened fists, all the while staring at Aaron, as if to ensure that he understood her.

The children were carefree; Celia was not. She was worried, and so was Mark. He'd attempted to make light of it this morning, but he had been unable to hide the concern in his eyes. Today he'd meet the hermit. Today he'd learn whether the old man was his father or simply an eccentric former miner. And, if Celia's prayers were answered, today Mark would relinquish his anger at his parents and—more importantly—at God. Though she'd been praying almost constantly since she had wakened, Celia still worried that Mark was not ready to open his heart. It was in the Lord's hands now. Celia knew that. That was one of the reasons she had brought the children outside, so she would be surrounded by the beauty of God's creation.

"I pull." Aaron tugged at her skirt to get her attention. When she nodded, he engaged in another of his routines, gripping the wagon's handle and yanking. Though he accomplished little, Aaron seemed to enjoy the exercise, and Emma never failed to giggle at the sight of her playmate pretending to be a horse.

Celia smiled indulgently at the children. She had been right in coming outside. The fresh air and Aaron's antics had helped her put aside her worries, leaving her able to breathe freely.

She glanced down the street, smiling again when she saw Bertha emerging from the parsonage. "Good morning."

"It is, isn't it?" Bertha tickled Emma's chin, then reached out to give Aaron a hug. When he took a step backward before extending his right hand, the minister's wife raised an eyebrow. "What's this?"

"I'm afraid it's something he learned from Mark. Ever since he saw him shake Doc's hand, Aaron wants to shake hands with everyone."

"How sweet." Solemnly, Bertha let the boy shake her hand, her lips twitching ever so slightly when he gave her hand a vigorous pumping. "Were you heading somewhere special?" she asked after Aaron released her hand and returned to chattering at Emma.

"I needed fresh air, and I thought Aaron might want to play on the swings." Though

Celia's front porch boasted a swing, it was more suited to courting couples than exuberant youngsters. Fortunately, the school yard held three simple board and rope swings, one of them close enough to the ground for Aaron's short legs.

As a gust of wind threatened Bertha's hat, she tightened the ribbons. "May I join you? I was on my way to the store for a few more items for Thanksgiving, but there's no rush."

Celia waited until Aaron was happily swinging before she turned to Bertha. The parson's wife had lifted Emma out of the wagon and was cooing to her as she cradled her in her arms. "I meant to tell you that I'm planning to bring oyster pudding as well as pound cake."

"Oysters?" Bertha raised an eyebrow. "That'll be a treat for us, but are you sure? They're very dear."

"The oysters were a gift." Celia pursed her lips, remembering the way they'd been presented. "From Frank," she added.

"I see." Though she adjusted Emma's hood so that only her eyes and nose were exposed, Bertha did not seem affected by the cold. Her green eyes sparkled with mirth, and her smile was as warm as a summer day. "I'm not surprised. Didn't I tell you he was courting you?"

It was futile to deny the truth. Even though the oysters had been a less than romantic gift, there was no ignoring the fact that Frank had presented them as a token of his affection. "The problem is, I don't want to be courted." *By him.* Though Bertha was a dear friend, Celia was not about to admit that her views on remarriage were changing, thanks to Mark.

"I know you're still grieving for Josef," Bertha said as she placed Emma back in the wagon, tucking the heavy blanket around her legs. "Your grief is natural, but you need to think about your future and Emma's."

It was a familiar refrain. Celia looked at Aaron. He wouldn't be happy about leaving the swing, but it was time the rest of them began to move. "I am thinking about the future," Celia said as she motioned to Aaron. "It's true that I still miss Josef. I imagine a part of me always will. He was a good man, and I wish he hadn't died so young. Most of all, I wish he'd been able to watch our daughter grow up."

Celia sighed. "Sometimes I ache, knowing that Josef suffered through the three babies we lost but never got to see Emma." She laid a hand on Emma's head, reassuring herself that this precious child with her father's curly hair was safe. "There are painful times," she said softly, "but it's not like it was at first. The horrible feeling of emptiness that filled me for so many months is gone."

Bertha's smile was radiant. "That's healing," the minister's wife said simply. "I'm thankful you've found it."

If only Mark could too.

"What do you think, Charcoal? It can't be much farther, can it?" Others might call it a sign of madness, but as he'd crisscrossed the country looking for his father, Mark had grown accustomed to talking to his horse. Charcoal didn't seem to mind, and it kept Mark's voice from growing hoarse with disuse. The gelding neighed, as if agreeing with him. The road had long since ended, but the path that Doc had indicated on his map was visible, thanks to the footprints in the snow. Though the main street of Easton was clear, the trees here kept the sun from reaching the ground and melting the snow. Fortunately for Mark, someone—probably the hermit himself—had passed this way since the last storm.

Mark gripped the reins. He was almost there. The sinking feeling in the pit of his stomach told him the moment of reckoning was close. The problem was, he wasn't ready. Perhaps he never would be. He'd thought about

Celia's words—oh, how he'd thought about them—but he wasn't convinced that anything good had come from his father's desertion, anything other than meeting Celia. Mark had to admit that life had been decidedly pleasant since he'd arrived in Easton, but that wasn't enough to make up for all the years without a father.

Celia would probably say that God didn't promise to even the score; all he promised was that something good would happen. The question was, would it be enough? Would his reunion with his father—if the hermit was indeed his father—heal the festering wounds Mark carried? He'd soon know.

"C'mon, Charcoal." An unexpected sense of urgency filled Mark. "We've got to find the hermit. The cabin must be close."

When he reached the small clearing, Mark reined in Charcoal and stared at what Doc had called a cabin. Perhaps it had been a cabin at one time, but now the best Mark could say was that it was a tumbledown shack. The roof was pocked with holes, and large chunks of chinking were missing from the log walls, making it barely habitable. It was clear that whoever was living here hadn't made a fortune in mining or ranching or any of the other things he'd attempted.

Mark swallowed deeply. Though he'd tried not to form expectations that might be dashed, when he'd thought of his father, he had not pictured a man living in poverty. He wanted to convince himself that this was not the cabin Doc had meant, that there was another, more prosperous one in the next clearing, but he couldn't. Doc had made it clear that there was only one cabin in these woods.

The smoke rising from the chimney told Mark someone was home or not far away. In minutes, perhaps only seconds, he would know whether his journey had ended and whether the old hermit was his father. Resolutely, he flicked the reins, urging Charcoal forward.

"Anyone home?" he called when he'd looped the reins over a branch.

Mark waited, wondering if he should climb the two steps and knock on the door. He was about to shout again when the door opened, revealing a man in a faded flannel shirt and worn coveralls. As the man emerged from the shadows of the house, Mark's heart stopped. There was no doubt about it. He'd found his father. Though the man looked older than the fifty-five Mark knew him to be, there was no mistaking his resemblance to the wedding portrait. This man was an aged version of the one who'd smiled at his bride twenty-seven years ago.

The man took a step toward him, and as he did Mark saw the confusion on his face. "Who are you?" he demanded, his voice harsh with apparent anger at being disturbed.

Mark opened his mouth to speak, but no words would come. He had waited for this moment for more than two years, and now that it had arrived, he couldn't form a single word. This tall, slightly stooped, gray-haired man was his father.

His father took another step forward, then stopped abruptly as blood drained from his face and the gray eyes so like Mark's own clouded. "Abe?" The name was little more than a whisper. "Abe?" The man shook his head. "You cain't be. Abe's dead."

It took a moment for the words to register. When they did, Mark gasped and stumbled back a step, suddenly aware of the frigid air, the scent of pine trees, and the sound of Charcoal's soft snorting. It was the same day it had been a minute ago. Nothing had changed, and yet everything had. "Abe's dead," the man had said. His father was gone, and with him Mark's dream of reconciliation. Whoever he was, this man who looked so much like Pa wasn't his father. His father was dead.

The man who was not Abe Williams cocked his head to one side. "Who are you?"

"I'm Mark Williams, Abe's son." At least the anguish inside Mark wasn't reflected in his voice. "Who are you?" Charcoal neighed, as if echoing the question.

The man took another step forward, standing at the edge of the top step and peering down at Mark. "Mark, you say? I reckon that's the name Abe gave his son. What're you doin' here?"

Chasing a dream, but Mark wouldn't admit that. "I've been looking for my father."

The man shook his head. Mark noticed that, while the hermit's hair was longer than fashionable and appeared to have been chopped with no regard for symmetry, it was clean. "'Fraid you're too late. Abe done got himself killed back ten years or so."

A clump of snow tumbled from the evergreen closest to the cabin, crumbling as it landed. One moment it was a firm ball, the next nothing more than scattered flakes. Mark took a deep breath, trying to calm his thoughts. One moment he'd thought he'd found his father, the next his dreams had shattered.

The hermit's words made sense, for the letters had stopped in '72. What made no sense was the presence of this man who looked so much like his father. But his father had no family—or so Mark had believed. "Who are you?" Mark repeated the question.

"Lionel Williams. Abe was my brother." The man scratched his head. "I reckon that makes you my nephew."

If the resemblance hadn't been so strong, Mark would have thought the man was lying, but as Ma used to say, blood will tell, and blood told Mark that the man was truthful. "I didn't know Pa had a brother."

The man coughed. "I ain't surprised. Grace never did like me. Claimed I was a bad influence." He coughed again. "C'mon in. Cain't stand around outside all day. A man'll catch his death of cold."

He swung around and stepped back into the house, leaving Mark to follow him. *An uncle*, Mark thought as he entered the cabin. *I have an uncle*. While questions whirled through his brain, his eyes assessed the shack, noting that the interior was as dilapidated as the exterior. The floorboards had shrunk, leaving gaps that allowed cold to seep inside, and the sole window hung askew, letting in the frigid air. A small table flanked by two chairs and a bed built into one wall were the only furnishings, while an iron stove served as both heat and a cooking surface.

Though the room was modest in size, Mark noted that it was clean, and whatever was cooking smelled delicious. Perhaps the cabin's condition was not the result of poverty but of an inability to perform the needed work. Lionel moved slowly, and the persistent cough could indicate a serious illness. That might have been why he'd summoned Doc.

"So, boy, how did you find me?" the man asked when he'd shuffled to the table and settled onto one of the chairs. "I didn't figure anybody be lookin' for me or Abe. We been gone a long time."

Mark pulled the other chair out and positioned it closer to the door. Though Lionel appeared to crave the stove's warmth, he wasn't cold. "I've been looking for my father for two years," he said, "ever since Ma died."

Lionel looked up, his eyes darkening. "Grace died? How'd it happen?"

"She just keeled over one day. Doc said she had a bad heart, but that was the first I heard of it." One of the ladies in town had claimed Ma had died of a broken heart, that she'd never gotten over losing her husband. When he'd found the letters, their envelopes worn from frequent handling, Mark had suspected the woman knew something he hadn't.

"I'm sorry for your loss." The words were

conventional, the voice brusque. Lionel tipped his head toward the stove. "Pour yourself a cup of coffee. It ain't bad. Made it fresh this morning." When Mark hesitated, he added, "You might get me one too. These old bones don't move as good as they used to."

When Lionel had taken several swallows, Mark leaned forward. He wasn't here to drink coffee but to have his questions answered. Though this man wasn't Pa, he had known him better than anyone. "Will you tell me about my father, how he lived and how he…" Mark stopped, not wanting to pronounce the final word.

Lionel had no such compunctions. "Died," he said flatly. "I reckon I can do that. It shore is peculiar, sittin' here with you. Makes me think Abe's still alive." He tipped the cup to his mouth and drank deeply. "Now, where should I start?"

"Ma used to say the beginning was a good place."

Lionel's chuckle turned into a coughing spasm. When it ended, he looked back at Mark. "You already know Abe was my brother. Used to call him Squirt on account of him being short. He was five years younger than me. Took him awhile to catch up, but he finally did. Wound up the same height.

Some folks figured us for twins." Leaning back in his chair, Lionel smiled at the memory. "I reckon we was twins in some ways, like being born with itchy feet. All folks had to do was tell either one of us about a new place, and we was on our way. It shore was good, travelin' together. Ain't nothin' in life that beats explorin' a new place." He closed his eyes, and Mark wondered if he was trying to relive a particular adventure. As the smile faded, Lionel looked at Mark. "It's in the blood, but I reckon you know that. That's what brung you all the way to Wyoming Territory."

Mark shook his head. "I came because I was looking for Pa. I've got to admit that I saw some beautiful places along the way, and there were times when I enjoyed the adventure, but the traveling life's not for me. I'm ready to settle down." As he turned away from his uncle's piercing gaze, Mark pictured Celia in the kitchen, an apron protecting her dress, her face smudged with flour, her lips curved in the sweetest of smiles as she looked down at her daughter. Nothing he had seen, not even the majestic mountains nor the harsh beauty of the high plains, could compare to that.

"Abe thought the same thing. That's why he married your ma. It didn't last long, though. I reckon it was less than a year. Then he felt the west wind blow, and he was itchin' to go again." Lionel held out his empty cup in a silent request for a refill. As Mark headed to the stove, his uncle continued. "I tell you, boy, your pa and me had some fine times. We never did find that pot of gold, and there was times when our stomachs was empty, but by and large, him and me had a good life." He took a slug of coffee, then leaned back in the chair, a smile wreathing his face. "As long as I live, I don't reckon I'll forget that day near Santa Fe…" His voice trailed off, and the smile tipped upside down.

"What's wrong?" The man who'd been smiling looked as if he'd lost his best friend. Perhaps he had.

Lionel's frown deepened. "I cain't think about Santa Fe without rememberin' how it all ended." He cupped his hands around the mug and leaned forward. "Your pa just couldn't pass up an adventure. When he heard tell about a box canyon so narrow a horse couldn't hardly fit in it, there weren't nothin' gonna keep him away. The next thing I knew, he was dead."

Mark had ridden into a box canyon in New Mexico, admiring the steep walls and the way sunlight barely made it to the canyon floor.

Had it been the same one where his father had died? "What happened?"

"Seems like there was outlaws holed up in that canyon. They musta thought Abe was part of a posse. He didn't have a chance. They gunned him down afore he could reach his rifle." Lionel closed his eyes as he winced. "Worst day of my life. July 17 of '72."

It made sense. The last letter had been dated in late June of that year. Mark nodded slowly. "Pa's been dead for almost ten and a half years, and we never knew." Though he hadn't intended it, his words sounded vaguely accusatory.

Lionel's eyes flew open and he glared at Mark. "I wrote your ma a letter." The glare faded as he said, "Musta gotten lost somehow."

"Ma might have burned it," Mark admitted, "but I doubt that. As far as I can tell, she kept all of Pa's letters." And not one had mentioned his brother. Was that because Pa had known his wife didn't care for Lionel? As he thought back to the places he'd stopped along the way, Mark realized that no one had mentioned that there were two men named Williams traveling together. Perhaps their memories had faded.

Lionel stared at the door for a moment. "Reckon things woulda been different if you'd seen my letter. You wouldn't have had to come all the way out here."

Nodding slowly, Mark considered his uncle's words. It was true that his life would have been different if he'd known of his father's death. In all likelihood, he would have remained in Ohio. Unbidden, Mark's stomach clenched as he remembered Celia challenging him to find evidence of God's plan. Was this part of it? If he hadn't left home, Mark would not have come to Easton, he would not have met Celia, and he would not be thinking about how to give her roses for Christmas. His life would have been different, all right. But better? He doubted that.

Celia noticed the change the instant Mark entered the house. Though his gait was the same, his smile for Emma as warm as ever, his eyes were different. The anger was gone, replaced by something she could not identify. It wasn't sorrow, but it wasn't peace, either. Though she wished he had returned early enough that she could ask him what had happened and whether the hermit was his father, Mark had arrived at the same time as Hiram and Jacob. She would have to wait until the other men left.

And so Celia sat at the foot of the table,

watching the fried chicken disappear as the platter made its way around the table and listening to the men discuss their work. When Frank crowed that business was better than ever, Jacob cited rumors of Christmas bonuses for all the miners. Both men seemed to think Celia should be impressed. Instead, her thoughts remained centered on the man at the opposite end of the table. Mark had been unusually quiet, lost in his own thoughts.

"What are you planning to do about Thanksgiving?" Frank directed his question to Jacob, perhaps because they were the only two talking. Even Aaron, who normally contributed a word or two, seemed more interested in eating than in conversation.

"What do you mean?" Jacob appeared perplexed. "My boy and I are gonna do the same thing we do every year. We're gonna attend services, then eat the best food of the year." Turning to Aaron, he raised an eyebrow. "Right, son?"

"Right, Pa." Aaron made a well in the middle of his mashed potatoes and waited for his father to fill it with gravy. "Mrs. Celia's gonna bake pound cake."

"I'm also taking oyster pudding," Celia said, giving Frank a little smile. Though he'd said nothing more, she imagined he was wondering when she would serve his gift.

His light blue eyes sparkled as he nodded. "Well, that settles it. I sure don't want to miss either of those." Once again, he leaned forward slightly, addressing Jacob. "What do you say we all go together?"

That wouldn't guarantee that Frank received a serving of oyster pudding, for it, like all the other foods that Easton's and Cedarville's women were bringing, would be placed on the table when the hostesses decided it was the right time. Celia had heard that arguments had broken out in previous years when the first people in line had a choice of every dish, leaving those at the end with little variety. In response, the organizers had decided that specialty foods would be added to the serving table one or two at a time.

Jacob shrugged. "I thought that was already decided. Folks go with their families, and we're Celia's family."

Celia tried not to bristle. Though Jacob had asked her to marry him, he was not her family. Not yet; probably not ever. Before she could speak, Hiram, who had been uncharacteristically silent, perhaps because fried chicken was his favorite meal, turned toward Celia. "Was that your plan?"

It hadn't been. Though she had assumed that Hiram and Mark, since they boarded with her, would accompany her and Emma to the celebration, Celia hadn't thought about Jacob and Frank joining them. Still, there was merit to the idea, for it would keep Frank from fussing, and so she nodded. The truth was, she didn't care who shared her Thanksgiving table. What mattered was what Mark had learned today.

Apparently mollified by Celia's agreement, Frank and Jacob did not linger after supper, and Hiram retired to his room earlier than normal. Celia said a silent prayer of thanks as she turned toward Mark. The dishes could wait. "Do you want to talk about what happened?"

He nodded and followed her into the parlor. When he settled into the chair that she had begun to think of as his own, he looked solemn. "The day didn't turn out the way I'd expected."

That sounded ominous. Perhaps it was the reason Celia had found his expression inscrutable. When Mark volunteered nothing more, she asked the question that had been foremost in her mind. "Is the hermit your father?"

Mark shook his head. "His brother. Pa was killed over ten years ago."

Killed, not died. Celia's heart welled with

compassion as she thought of the pain that announcement must have caused. It was sad enough, watching a loved one die from illness as her parents had. Sudden death was more difficult, for there was no opportunity for farewells. But in either case, Mark had not been there. His dream of knowing his father would never be realized. "I don't know what to say. 'Sorry' seems inadequate."

Mark's eyes darkened until they were almost black. "I should have figured it out when I saw that the letters stopped, but it was still a shock." He ran a hand through his hair, as if in frustration. "I've spent two years searching, and what do I have to show for it? The thing that drove me, the hope of getting to know my father, is gone. Now I have nothing."

Anger might not have returned, but Celia heard the despair in Mark's voice and knew that was equally painful. "You do have something, Mark. You have the truth. Now you know that you don't have to search any longer. You can plan your future." And maybe, just maybe, that future would include Easton.

His eyes were bleak as he looked at Celia. "For a moment when I was in the hermit's cabin—my uncle's cabin," he corrected himself, "I thought you were right and that maybe something good would come out of this, but as

I rode home, the truth came crashing in. It was supposed to set me free, but I don't feel that way. I feel as if I've lost my father." Mark's laugh held no mirth. "Isn't that crazy? I never had him, so how could I lose him? But I have. I've lost everything."

Celia understood, for that was how she had felt when Josef had died. With both of her parents gone, she had been bereft of family, sustained only by the knowledge that she was expecting Josef's child. Though Emma had not yet been born, her presence had comforted Celia, reminding her that she was not alone. Mark might not recognize it, but he wasn't alone either.

"You've lost a lot," Celia admitted, "but you've also gained something. You learned that you have an uncle. You're not alone, Mark. He's your family."

The knowledge appeared to bring no comfort.

Chapter Eight

"Why don't you and Emma come with me? I've got the wagon hitched."

Mark stood in the doorway of the kitchen, watching while Celia put the final jar into the basket she'd prepared. When she had heard about his uncle, she had volunteered to send a supply of home-cooked meals the next time Mark visited. Though she had wanted to help the older man, there had been another equally important reason for her offer: she wanted Mark to spend more time with his uncle. Perhaps he would realize that he was not alone and that something good had come from his search.

Celia frowned as she looked down. Laden with two buckets of fried chicken, a pot of green beans simmered with bacon, several loaves of bread, and an assortment of jams and pickles, the basket was almost filled. All that remained was to top it with the now-cool pound cake. The food was ready. She was not. Though she'd thought of Lionel Williams frequently in the three days since Mark had told her of his existence, not once had Celia considered delivering the food to him.

"I don't think that's a good idea," she said firmly. "There's a reason your uncle lives alone." It was one thing for his nephew to visit, quite another to bring an unknown woman and her child with him.

Mark crooked an eyebrow as he regarded Celia. "Maybe the reason isn't the one you think. Maybe he's alone because of circumstances, not choice. Until I showed up at his cabin, he had no family."

Something in Mark's voice told Celia he had invited her for another reason: he was reluctant to go alone. Whatever words had been exchanged—or perhaps it was the ones that had been left unspoken—Mark was not comfortable returning to his uncle's home. He needed her help. Celia looked around the kitchen, considering. Aaron was spending the day with Bertha; supper would not require lengthy preparation; cleaning the house could wait until tomorrow. There was no reason not to go, and judging from Mark's expression, at least one very good reason to bundle Emma into warm clothes, grab her own coat, and climb into the wagon he'd rented from the livery.

"All right," she said with a smile, "but if your uncle seems uncomfortable with Emma and me there, we'll stay in the wagon."

Five minutes later, Celia was settled on the plank seat next to Mark, Emma perched on her lap. For once, her daughter was content to simply sit and stare at her surroundings. It was her first excursion in a wagon, and Emma seemed fascinated by both the horse and the speed with which they were moving. She gurgled and babbled, occasionally batting her fists against her legs. As Celia watched, she discovered that when Mark tugged on the reins, Emma tried to imitate him.

"I think Emma wants to learn to handle a horse," Celia told him. "Look how she follows your movements." But Emma had lost interest, and her slowly closing eyes signaled she would soon be asleep. Celia hoped a long nap would mean that her daughter would not be cranky when they arrived, for it was unlikely that Mark's uncle had much experience with infants.

As Emma drifted off to sleep, Celia studied her surroundings. In the twelve years that she had lived in Easton, she had never been this far out of town. The trees were thicker here, encroaching on the track they followed, leaving the ground sun-dappled. The clumps of snow that decorated the tips of the evergreen boughs left no doubt that, though the calendar might disagree, winter had come to Wyoming. Wagon wheels crunched on the snow, while the horse whinnied occasionally. They were ordinary noises, as comforting as the soft sound of her daughter's breathing. As a mantle of peace settled over her, Celia looked at the man who sat only inches away. He was not at peace, for the angle of his jaw and the way he clutched the reins betrayed his tension.

"You don't want to visit him, do you?" Celia kept her voice low, not wanting to disturb Emma.

Mark's eyes widened. "I didn't realize it was so obvious, but you're right. It's silly, but I hardly slept last night for worrying about Lionel."

"It's not silly. It's normal. Your uncle gave you some very unwelcome news. It's only natural to be reluctant to see him."

Mark nodded. "I'm not sure he wants to see me again. I'm not even sure I want to see him."

"I'm not surprised." Celia's gaze was caught

by a flash among the trees, a deer or perhaps an antelope seeking shelter until the intruders had passed. At another time, she would have stopped, hoping to identify the animal. Now she cared only about helping Mark. There had to be some way to comfort him.

As the image of Easton's church flickered into her brain, Celia nodded. That was the answer. Giving Mark a small smile, she said, "You and your uncle are connected strangers. That's always awkward at the beginning." When Mark raised a questioning eyebrow, she continued. "You've just met and you don't know much about each other, so you're still strangers. At the same time, you're connected by your father, and that makes you feel as if you ought to get to know each other, even though you might not have otherwise." Mark's nod encouraged Celia to continue. "You're pulled apart by the fact that you're strangers, but at the same time, the connection is drawing you together. The tug-of-war can be uncomfortable."

"You're right about that," Mark agreed. "It is uncomfortable. But how do you know about connected strangers? I've never heard that term."

"I hadn't either until Reverend Pearson's sermon last month. He said all of us in the congregation were strangers at one point. What brought us together and ultimately kept us together was that we were connected by our Father. Our heavenly Father, that is."

Though she hadn't expected it to happen so quickly, Mark's shoulders began to relax. "It's an interesting idea," he said. And, judging from his expression, one he found more appealing than their discussion of Romans 8:28.

"The parson's a wise man." Hoping she had judged Mark's mood correctly, Celia continued. "I wish you'd come to services with Hiram and me. No matter how worried I am, I always find peace there."

She had been mistaken. Though Mark nodded, his shoulders stiffened again. "I'm glad for you, Celia. Truly, I am, but church isn't for me." The finality of his tone left no doubt that he considered the discussion at an end.

He gestured toward the right. "See the smoke?" A plume rose above the trees. "We're almost there."

Moments later the wagon entered a small clearing. Celia stared at the source of the smoke, feeling the blood drain from her face as she saw the condition of Lionel Williams's home. "I thought you said your uncle lived in a cabin." She turned to Mark, wondering if the dilapidated building was part of the reason for his reluctance to return. "That's a hut."

"It could use a few repairs," he said with a wry smile. "That's why I hired the wagon. I brought my tools and some materials. I hope Lionel will accept my help. He needs it, but he's a stubborn, independent man."

Just like Mark.

With the basket of food in his hand, Mark escorted Celia and Emma toward the cabin, calling out, "Lionel. Uncle Lionel."

Only seconds later the door opened, and a tall, gray-haired man stepped outside. "I ain't deaf, boy. I heard you comin'." Though the voice was harsher than Mark's, there was no mistaking the resemblance. Even if she hadn't been told his identity, Celia would have known this man was related to Mark. It appeared, however, that he lacked Mark's carpentry skills, or he would have repaired his home.

Apparently unconcerned by his surroundings, Lionel Williams turned his attention to Celia. "Now, who's this? You didn't tell me you had a wife and baby."

Celia felt the blood rush to her cheeks, but before she could correct him, Mark laid his free hand on her shoulder. "This is Mrs.

Anderson and her daughter, Emma. Mrs. Anderson is my landlady," he added.

Lionel Williams's face softened into what might have passed for a smile. "C'mon in, Miz Anderson. It ain't often a purty gal visits me." He held the door open and ushered Celia inside.

At least it was clean, Celia realized as her eyes adjusted to the darkness. That was the best she could say about Mr. Williams's abode. The condition of the interior was even worse than the exterior had led her to expect, with shafts of light from holes in the roof giving the floor a polka-dot pattern. Though the single room was warm, the stove would require frequent feeding to combat the cold coming through the missing chinks in the log walls, and she could feel a breeze from the window. It was no wonder Mark had come prepared for repairs.

"Have a seat." The older man gestured toward the table and its two chairs before dragging a crate to the other side of the table. "You can sit here, boy," he told Mark.

Mark gave Celia a brief nod but said nothing, leaving her to provide an explanation for their visit.

"I thought you might enjoy not having to cook for a few days, so we brought you some food." She stressed the plural pronoun, wanting the older man to include Mark in his thanks.

But he did not. "Thank you, ma'am." Mr. Williams gave her a smile as he removed the basket's lid. His smile widened as the aromas of chicken and fresh bread filled the cabin. "That smells mighty good, ma'am. Doc brings me supplies when he comes, and I'm pretty good with a rifle, so I never go hungry. Truth is, though, I get tired of my own cookin' and my company."

Celia caught Mark's eye and nodded. He had been right. His uncle was solitary by circumstance, not design. "Have you thought about moving into town?" she asked. "There are a lot of friendly people there."

Before Mr. Williams could reply, Emma started to fuss. Since it was her "I'm tired of being held" fussing, Celia placed her on the floor and handed her the wooden spoon that was her favorite toy this week. Once again content, Emma began to coo and gurgle, apparently holding a conversation with her spoon.

Mr. Williams said nothing, merely stared at Emma as if she were a new species. Perhaps she was. Though Mark's travels had brought him into contact with small children, it was possible that his father and uncle had had primarily adult male companionship, and for however long he'd lived here, Mr. Williams would have had no companions. Surely he'd be happier living in town.

As if he'd read her thoughts, Mark expanded on Celia's suggestion. "Mrs. Anderson runs a mighty fine boardinghouse. You wouldn't have to cook at all if you lived there."

Wrenching his gaze from Emma and her spoon, the older man shook his head. "No offense, ma'am, but there's too many folks in Easton for me. Why, Doc said you're up to 150 now. With that many, a man couldn't turn around without bumpin' into someone else. No, ma'am, that's not the place for me. I'm comfortable right here."

When Celia glanced at Mark, she saw that his lips were threatening to turn upward, as if he were slightly amused by his uncle's response. He kept his voice neutral as he said, "You'd be more comfortable if the wind didn't blow through the cracks and the snow stayed outside."

That got an immediate response. Mr. Williams straightened his back and glared at Mark. "You criticizing my home, boy?"

Mark shook his head. "Simply stating a fact. I told Mrs. Anderson I didn't think you'd want to move, so I brought some boards and a ladder. I was hoping you'd let me repair your roof."

For a moment the two men stared at each other, and Celia had the impression they were communicating without words. At last, Mr. Williams nodded. "That's mighty generous of you, Mark. I cain't say no to that offer." Mr. Williams shook his head, and his face reddened ever so slightly. "I hate to admit it, but I'm gettin' too old to climb up on the roof." He glanced at the window and cocked his head to one side, as if listening for something. "Looks like a fine day to go on the roof. For once, that blasted wind ain't blowin', so I won't have no worries about you gettin' blowed off. But we oughta eat first." He made a show of sniffing the air before he grinned at Celia. "Forgit about movin' into town. If this tastes as good as it smells, I may just keep you here."

The meal was more pleasant than Celia had dared hope, with both Mark and his uncle keeping the conversation flowing. To her relief, Mark's earlier wariness appeared to have dissipated, and his uncle seemed to enjoy the company, even when Emma began to cry. Though she knew he'd deny it, Celia suspected that the older man was lonely but too proud to admit it. Before the pound cake was served, she resolved that, one way or another, Mark's uncle would not spend Christmas alone.

"A meal like that makes a man think about napping, not crawling on a roof," Mark said as he laid his fork on his now-empty plate. When they were headed back to town, he would thank Celia again and again, not just for the best meal he suspected his uncle had eaten in months but for accompanying him. He knew she hadn't wanted to come, and he had seen her concern over the cabin's poor condition, but having her and Emma here had smoothed the rough moments, helping Mark and his uncle establish an amicable relationship.

"C'mon, Mark. Naps are for babies," Lionel declared. "Let's let Miz Anderson put her daughter to sleep. She don't want her fussin' when her pa gets home."

Mark heard Celia's quick intake of breath, but before he could correct his uncle's mistaken belief, she spoke. "Emma's father died before she was born. He was killed in the mine."

"Oh." Lionel's gaze moved from Celia to Emma and back again. "I'm mighty sorry, ma'am. I had no way of knowin'. Sorry," he repeated.

Not wanting to dwell on Celia's loss, Mark led the way outside, pulling the ladder from the wagon and propping it against the house. Though no one would call it a warm day, at least there had been no fresh snow overnight and the sun had melted the ice from the roof.

"I'll hold the end," his uncle said, inspecting the ladder while Mark began to gather his tools. "I shore wouldn't want you to fall. I reckon Miz Anderson would be mighty upset if that was to happen." He grabbed one of the boards Mark had brought and carried it to the foot of the ladder. "She's a mighty fine woman, Miz Anderson is," Lionel said as he laid the plank on the ground. "A woman like her could make even a man with itchy feet think about settlin' down. I reckon that's what happened to Abe."

Mark didn't like the direction the conversation was heading. He was here to repair his uncle's cabin. If he started thinking about his parents, who knew what might happen? He could tumble off the roof. But he couldn't let his uncle's statement go unchallenged. "Celia's not like my mother."

"Oh, I don't know. They're both mighty fine-lookin' women. That could turn a man's head." Lionel put a hand on Mark's shoulder, keeping him from climbing the ladder.

"I reckon you don't want an old man's advice, but I'm gonna give it, anyhow. Don't make the same mistake your ma and pa did. They should never a' done what they did—get themselves hitched, then live apart."

Although Mark agreed, his uncle was simplifying the story. Tugging the brim of his hat to block the sun's rays, Mark said, "Ma didn't have a choice."

"You think so? We all got choices. Even your ma. Abe begged her to come with us. He waited 'til you was born, hopin' she'd change her mind, but Grace was too scared of the unknown to take a chance." When Mark started to protest, Lionel held up a restraining hand. "I ain't sayin' Abe was right, either. All I know is, it were a downright shame that two folks who loved each other the way they did spent their whole lives apart."

While he tugged his hat brim to shield his eyes from the sun, Mark's mind seized on one part of his uncle's speech. "You think they loved each other?" If they had, perhaps that was the reason Ma had not remarried. That was far more palatable than the idea that she had considered her marriage a mistake or that she'd had suitors who would have been poor fathers.

Lionel's expression said the answer should

have been obvious. "Sakes alive, yes. Problem was, neither one was willin' to bend. They shore was two stubborn folks." He pointed his finger at Mark. "I hope to heavens you ain't like that."

Some might claim Mark was stubborn in his refusal to stop searching for his father. "I might be. I don't know."

Lionel squinted, as if trying to see within Mark's heart. "I'm gonna give you some more advice. Don't let Miz Anderson slip away from you. Gals like that don't come along but once in a lifetime." His eyes narrowed even more. "And don't go tellin' me you don't care. I can see in your eyes that you do."

"I do care about her." Mark wondered if his uncle was as surprised as he was that he had revealed that. Here he was, telling a stranger about his deepest feelings. And yet, perhaps it was because Lionel wasn't simply a stranger but what Celia had called a connected stranger.

"If things were different, I might be courting her," Mark admitted.

Lionel grabbed another board from the wagon. When he had laid it next to the others, he frowned at Mark. "How different do they need to be? Seems to me, if you care about Miz Anderson, you oughta ask her to marry you. What's the problem? What's gotta be different?"

Mark wondered how much his bachelor uncle would understand. "There's more than Celia to think about. There's Emma too. She deserves a good pa." And that was the problem. "How could I be that when I don't know anything about being a father—good or bad? It's not as if I had an example to follow."

Lionel was silent for a moment, as if considering Mark's concerns. "You could learn," he said at last.

He made it sound simple, but it wasn't. Just as not everyone could be a carpenter, Mark knew not everyone could be a good father.

"That would mean risking Emma's happiness. I'm not willing to do that." She would be better off with a man who'd proven himself as a father, a man like Jacob. That was what Emma needed. Wasn't it?

"That was the best oyster pudding I ever ate." Hiram smacked his lips to emphasize his words. "I hope you'll make it again next Thanksgiving."

"I agree," Mark chimed in. "It was definitely the best I've ever eaten. Of course"— his lips turned up—"it was also the only oyster pudding I've ever eaten."

As he'd probably intended, Celia laughed. "I'm not sure whether I should be flattered or not."

The two men had remained at the table after the rest of the guests had dispersed to stand in corners, talking, smoking, and taking occasional surreptitious swigs from the jugs of spirits that someone had smuggled into the church. The forbidden whiskey was as much a part of Easton's Thanksgiving tradition as the succulent foods.

When Hiram rose to join the smokers, Mark moved to the seat on Celia's right. Emma lay sleeping in a basket on her other side, despite the almost deafening sounds of close to two hundred people talking. Now that her daughter was asleep, Celia could eat dessert. It had been a challenge, holding Emma while she ate dinner, and though she had a cup of coffee and a piece of pie in front of her, Celia had yet to taste it.

"Be flattered," Mark said. "The pudding was very good, and your pound cake was even better than the one you made for Lionel. He talks about that every time I visit."

Celia's smile broadened. In the few hours she'd spent with him, she'd become fond of the gruff old man. That was why she was glad that Mark continued to visit him, even though it meant that she saw Mark less often. The trips into the forest took time he could ill afford, and with Christmas approaching, he had no recourse but to spend his evenings in the workshop. It was a major concession that he'd come to the Thanksgiving celebration today, and even then, he'd only agreed to join Easton's and Cedarville's citizens for dinner. Though he'd claimed work as an excuse for not attending the worship service, Celia was certain that was not his only reason. As far as she knew, he'd not set foot inside the church.

"Have you convinced your uncle to spend Christmas with us?" When she'd mentioned the idea to Mark, he'd agreed that it was a good one and had offered to try to persuade Mr. Williams.

Mark shook his head. "I think he's weakening, but he's still refusing."

Celia took a bite of pie. Unlike the men, who had insisted on having pieces of her pound cake, she had chosen a wedge of Bertha's apple pie for her dessert. "Do you suppose bribery would work?"

Mark's lips twitched with amusement. "I don't know. What did you have in mind?"

"Tell him I'll serve pound cake for dinner *and* I'll make an extra one just for him."

Amusement turned into laughter. "I wouldn't be surprised if that seals the deal."

When Emma started to fuss again, Celia gathered her into her arms and rose. Sometimes just pacing back and forth soothed her daughter. She smiled, looking down at the child who had brought such happiness to her life. Though Emma would not remember it, her first Thanksgiving had been a success by anyone's standards. The parson's sermon about gratitude had helped Celia recognize that although the past year had brought many changes to her life, most of them had been good ones. She had spent the rest of the day following Reverend Pearson's advice and had counted her blessings.

There had been many today, with good company and good food high on the list. Frank had been pleased when the oyster pudding was available as their group made their way through the line. It wasn't coincidence, Celia was certain, but the result of Bertha's careful planning, and that gave her another reason to give thanks—for friends like Bertha. The only problem had been Emma. Celia's normally gregarious daughter seemed anxious today. The reason could be, as one of the other mothers had suggested, the presence of all the strangers. Celia hoped that was the case, for it was far better than the possibility that Emma had contracted another illness.

Mark stretched out his arms. "Let me hold her. You deserve to enjoy your pie. Emma will be fine with me for a couple minutes."

She would. Celia knew that. "Thank you," she said as she sat down on the bench. "Give me five minutes."

Nodding, Mark carried Emma toward the door. Since he'd grabbed the blanket, he was probably planning to take her outside for a few minutes.

Celia had just taken a bite of pie when Aaron clambered onto the bench next to her. Though the boy had eaten his meal with the rest of the group, as soon as he'd finished, he'd joined the other children for games in the far corner of the room. She hadn't expected him to return.

"I love you, Mrs. Celia," Aaron announced, throwing his arms around her neck. "I want you to be my ma."

Celia's heart lurched, and she almost choked on her pie. Though she wouldn't have put it past Jacob to have coached his son, it seemed unlikely he had spoken to Aaron since they'd left the table, since he was talking with the men in the opposite corner from the children.

The boy's words had come from the heart, and that made them all the more poignant.

"I love you too," Celia said, pressing Aaron's head to her shoulder.

Though she had more than four weeks before she had to give Jacob his answer, the question was never far from her mind. When he'd first proposed, Celia had not imagined that she might seriously consider marrying Jacob, and yet—though she had thought it impossible—the idea was less repugnant than it had once been. The difference was Mark. Listening to his stories and realizing how greatly the absence of a father had affected him had led Celia to agree with Bertha. Emma did need a father. Celia couldn't bear the thought that twenty years from now, her daughter might tell a stranger that Celia hadn't given her the one thing she wanted most: a father.

Emma needed a father. Aaron needed a mother. Jacob was right. Their marriage would be good for the children. The problem was, she did not want Jacob as her husband. She wanted Mark.

Celia blinked furiously, trying to keep the tears that welled in her eyes from falling. There was no point in wishing for something that wouldn't happen. Even though Mark might stay in Easton past the winter, he was not a man she could marry. No matter how much she cared for him—and Celia would not deny that Mark had touched emotions deep inside her—she could not entrust Emma's future to a man who was so angry with God. Josef's death was proof that life could end in an instant and that Celia needed to provide for Emma's future in case she wasn't there to share it. That led her back to Jacob. He would be a good father for Emma. He was steady and God-fearing.

Celia sighed. Those qualities were important. The problem was, they weren't enough. She wanted love.

Chapter Nine

He'd made a mistake.

Mark took a deep breath, exhaling slowly. It was a technique he had learned to help him relax. Unfortunately, today it accomplished nothing. He was not calm. Far from it. The only thing he wanted was to turn around and flee, but he couldn't do that. That would be the act of a coward, and he wasn't a coward. Just as importantly, he was carrying Emma, and he couldn't leave with her.

He took another breath, this time focusing on Emma's face. The little girl nestled so close to him giggled. Ever since Thanksgiving dinner, every time he'd come into the room, she had held up her arms, signaling that she wanted him to hold her. Celia had laughed, telling Mark he had a new admirer, but he hadn't minded. The truth was, it felt good. When he held Emma, he felt as if his life had a purpose. It might be nothing more important than keeping a baby from crying, but he couldn't deny the sense of satisfaction he found in knowing that he was needed.

Perhaps that was the reason he'd agreed when Celia had urged him to attend the first Advent service with her and Emma. That and the fact that he hadn't wanted to disappoint Celia again. She made no secret of the fact that her faith was important to her, just as she hadn't disguised her disappointment when Mark had refused to accompany her to church on Thanksgiving. Celia had done so much for him, especially where Lionel was concerned, that he wanted to repay her. He had thought an hour in church wouldn't be too difficult. Now he wasn't certain.

As if she had heard his thoughts, Celia gave him an encouraging smile. "I'm glad you're here," she said softly, "and I'm glad you're holding Emma. She's getting heavy."

Mark nodded as they climbed the steps. Perhaps this wouldn't be as bad as he feared. He'd concentrate on Celia and Emma and not on the fact that he was entering a place where his welcome was unsure. "Emma weighs less than a log."

"But logs don't squirm. My daughter definitely does." Celia led the way into the sanctuary, stopping at the last pew. "I used to sit in front, but now I sit back here," she explained. "That way, if Emma gets fussy, I can take her outside."

"That's fine with me." If he felt uncomfortable, he could leave without disturbing too many people.

When Celia took her seat, Mark handed Emma to her and was surprised when she placed the child on the pew between them. Though Emma's legs stuck straight out, she didn't appear uncomfortable. Instead, she bounced up and down, apparently enjoying the wooden seat, and when a young couple with a baby settled in the pew before them, Emma grinned and cooed at the other infant. This wasn't the way Mark remembered church. Services had always been somber, and no one—not even a baby—would dare to smile.

The church was not what he'd expected, either. He hadn't paid much attention to it on Thanksgiving, when it had been turned into a dining hall for close to two hundred people. Then the focus had been on food and conversation. Today, with the pews back in place, it was once more a house of worship. It was simpler than the church in Ohio, devoid of stained-glass windows and an elaborately carved altar and pulpit. Though some might call it stark, the simplicity appealed to Mark. By the time the bell pealed, the sanctuary was filled. The rustling of skirts, the clomp of boots, and the whispered conversations ended abruptly as Reverend Pearson took his place in front of the altar and announced the first hymn.

Mark rose with the rest of the congregation, nodding when Celia opened the hymnal and offered to share it with him. He didn't know the song. Even if he had, he couldn't hold a tune, but that didn't seem to matter. No one looked askance when he attempted to sing the second verse, his voice coming out as little more than a croak. Celia kept singing, her voice clear and true, her face so filled with joy that Mark felt a pang of jealousy pierce his heart. What must it be like, to feel so happy? She was a widow with an infant, struggling to keep her home, and yet she appeared as carefree as a child. Though she had told Mark that she found a special peace here, he had not expected that peace to be so evident.

When the last notes faded away and the congregation took their seats, Mark let out a breath of relief. Since God hadn't showered him with fire and brimstone, he must not be angry that Mark was in his house, and the little smiles Celia sent his way told him that she was still pleased he had come. Mark sat back, relaxing when Emma held out her arms, indicating that she wanted to be held again. By the time the minister climbed the few steps into the pulpit, Mark was no longer feeling out of place.

Reverend Pearson stood silently for a moment, his eyes moving slowly around the sanctuary, as if he were a shepherd counting his flock. Though his gaze met Mark's briefly, the minister gave no sign of surprise at Mark's presence, merely continued his tally. Then he bowed his head for a moment before nodding at his parishioners. "Advent is a time of preparation," Reverend Pearson said, his voice deeper and more resonant than it was in ordinary conversation. "We prepare ourselves for Christmas and the celebration of the greatest gift we will ever receive—the gift of our Savior." He paused as the congregation murmured sounds of assent. "When we think of preparation for that blessed event, we usually think of Mary and the plans she made for the birth of her son. How often do we remember that Mary was not alone?"

The parson paused again. This time there was an uncomfortable rustling, as if the parishioners were uncertain what he meant. "When we arrange our nativity scenes, we include the figure of Joseph, but how often do we think about him? Joseph had preparations of his own. He had to prepare for the coming of a child who was not his. How do you think he felt?" Without waiting for a response, the minister said, "We know that he was fearful, for St. Matthew tells us Joseph was visited by an angel of the Lord who told him not to fear. Can you imagine what his fears must have been? Before the angel appeared in a dream, Joseph knew only that the woman he had planned to marry was carrying a child who was not his."

Somewhere in the front of the church, a man cleared his throat, and a woman whispered to the white-haired matron by her side. Reverend Pearson waited until the church was once again silent before he continued. "I imagine Joseph was shamed by that knowledge, but how must he have felt when he learned, and I quote from the gospel of St. Matthew, 'that which is conceived in her is of the Holy Ghost'? Though the angel told him not to fear, I suspect Joseph's fears were multiplied by the angel's announcement. He was only a human. How would he raise a son who was divine?

How would any man be able to shoulder that responsibility?"

Once again the minister paused, letting his words register. "Joseph could have put Mary aside. He could have done what Pontius Pilate did and washed his hands of this child, but he did not. Joseph trusted God to show him the way, and that trust helped him overcome his fears. Because of Joseph and his faith, Jesus had both an earthly and a heavenly Father. He had brothers and sisters. He was part of a family, all because one man overcame his fears. What an example he set for all of us!"

Tears pricked the back of Mark's eyes as the minister continued to speak. Had Reverend Pearson known he would be here today? It seemed unlikely, for he hadn't made the decision until this morning, and yet the sermon appeared to have been written specifically for him. Like Joseph, he was riddled with fears, many of them centered on the child who was even now sleeping in his arms.

The parson was right. Mark had never wondered about Joseph and his role in the nativity, but now he couldn't stop thinking of the man who'd been born almost two thousand years ago. It was true Mark's life wasn't the same as Joseph's. After all, Emma was a human child. But he shared some of the same fears that Jesus's earthly father had. The question was, could Mark overcome them? Could he be like Joseph? And even if he could, would he find the same peace Celia had? Mark wanted that, more than anything he could recall, but he didn't know how to begin.

Somehow he got through Sunday dinner, although afterward he could not recall what Celia had served. He must have participated in the conversation, for no one looked at him askance. But while he was going through the motions of a normal Sunday, Mark's thoughts were whirling. He had dozens of questions, and there was only one person who could help him with answers. As soon as he could, he slipped away from the boardinghouse, hoping Reverend Pearson would be at home.

To Mark's relief, when he knocked at the parsonage door, the minister opened it. Now there was only one more hurdle. "If this is an inconvenient time, I can come back later."

"Not at all." Reverend Pearson shook his head. Though he no longer wore his clerical robe and stole, his demeanor was different from the time he'd visited Mark's workshop. It was as if he knew why Mark had come. "Come in." The minister led Mark to the parlor and gestured toward one of the chairs that flanked the stove. "I'll be back in a moment. I want to tell Bertha we're not to be interrupted."

When the parson returned and took his seat, Mark spoke. "I'm not here to discuss your wife's blanket chest."

Though his face remained sober, there was a hint of mirth in the older man's brown eyes. "I didn't think you were. If I had to guess, I would say this has something to do with the fact that you attended services this morning." The minister smiled as Mark nodded. "I was glad to see you there."

"Did you know that I was coming?" Mark posed one of the questions that had been chasing through his brain. "Is that why you preached about Joseph and his fears?"

The minister shook his head. "'No' to both questions. Each week I pray for guidance when I start to prepare my sermon. Sometimes the ideas come easily, but this week wasn't one of those times. When I opened my Bible, searching for inspiration, and saw the verses in St. Matthew about the angel appearing to Joseph in a dream, I knew that would be my subject."

Mark swallowed deeply. "I've heard hundreds of sermons, but there's never been one like this. I felt as if you had written it for me alone." He looked at the minister. It couldn't be coincidence that he'd delivered this particular sermon today. Celia had claimed there were no coincidences. If she was right, this must have been part of God's plan. Though the room was warm, Mark shivered. He'd thought his presence in church might have drawn fire and brimstone. Instead, he'd found hope, and that sent shivers down his spine.

"I can't stop thinking about what you said. I know I'm like Joseph. I'm afraid I'm not good enough to raise a child. I want to, but I don't know how. All I know is I can't do it alone." The words tumbled like water over a falls, surprising Mark with their intensity. He hadn't been this honest, not even with Lionel.

Reverend Pearson leaned forward, his eyes as solemn as they'd been during the sermon. "None of us can do it alone. It's only our foolish pride that makes us think we can. Fortunately for us, God will help. All we have to do is ask."

The pastor made it sound simple, but Mark knew it wasn't. "I haven't trusted God in years—maybe never. Why would he want to help me?" That was the fear that had lodged deep inside him ever since he'd heard the minister's sermon, making all his other fears seem insignificant. Mark wanted help, but he knew he didn't deserve it.

"It's not a matter of deserving. God will help you because he loves you." The parson kept his eyes focused on Mark. "Think about someone you love. Do you stop loving them when they do something you don't like or even when they ignore you?"

"No." One of the things Mark had realized since he'd come to Easton was that the anger he had felt toward his mother had faded. He loved her, he had always loved her, even though he didn't agree with all of her decisions.

"God doesn't stop his love, either. All he asks is that we invite him into our hearts." The minister stretched his hand out to lay it on top of Mark's. "All you have to do is ask."

Though Reverend Pearson's hand was cool, his touch sent warmth flowing through Mark's veins. "Here? Now?" Surely something this important had to be done in a church. After all, that was God's house.

The minister nodded. "There's no better time or place." As if he had heard Mark's thoughts, he added, "God doesn't just meet us in church." Reverend Pearson withdrew his hand and rose. "I'll leave you alone for a while. Call out if you need me."

When the door was closed, Mark looked around. Other than the cross that hung on one wall, this could have been any house in Easton. Was the parson right? Was God here? There was only one way to know. Slowly Mark sank to his knees and stared at the cross.

"Dear God, I don't know what to say. I know I don't deserve your love, but I want it. I want you to guide me the way you guided Joseph. Show me what I should do next. Help me overcome my fears. I can't do it alone, but I know that you can do anything. Help me."

Mark closed his eyes and bowed his head, waiting for an answer, but there was none. No angels appeared to him. No voices spoke from clouds or burning bushes. There was nothing. And yet, as he knelt there, something changed. He felt as if an enormous weight had been lifted from his shoulders, leaving in its place the gentle, featherweight touch of peace.

Celia breathed in deeply. The house smelled of cinnamon, one of her favorite aromas. When Bertha had offered to keep Aaron one day a week so that Celia could finish her Christmas preparations without a young child underfoot, she had decided to make a batch of mulled apple cider as a thank-you for the Pearsons. She would deliver it along with Aaron.

"All right, sweetie," Celia said to her daughter when the jar of cider was cocooned in a towel, "we're going for a ride." Emma cooed, and Aaron grabbed his coat, managing to tangle the sleeves when he tried to put it on. "It's okay, Aaron. I won't leave you behind. You can help me pull the wagon." Fortunately, though it had been a week since the Thanksgiving celebration, the boy had said nothing more about wanting Celia to be his mother. That was good, for although she prayed about it every day, Celia was no closer to knowing how to resolve her dilemma. In less than a month, Jacob would expect her answer, and she was still torn between her conviction that both Aaron and Emma deserved two parents and her reluctance to marry for any reason other than love.

She walked slowly down the street, matching her pace to Aaron's as he chattered to Emma while attempting to pull the wagon. Unlike Celia, who preferred to spend winters indoors, the boy loved the cold and would stay outside until his lips turned blue, if she'd allow it. She would have to warn Bertha about that, for she had no doubt that Aaron would try to cajole Bertha into letting him play outdoors.

As they approached the parsonage, Celia's smile broadened at the sight of Mark leaving the church. She hadn't realized he wasn't still in his workshop, although, now that she thought about it, the outbuilding had been silent when she'd left the house. As far as Celia knew, last Sunday had been the first time Mark had set foot inside the church other than Thanksgiving dinner. Though she had longed to ask for his reaction, he had said nothing about the service at dinner that day, and they had had no private time since then. But, while he had not spoken of it, Celia knew that something had changed, for Mark looked different. The pain that he had never managed to hide completely was gone, replaced by what could only be called peace.

Celia increased her pace, eager to speak to Mark. "I thought you were working," she said when she had greeted him.

"I was," he admitted. Turning his head and speaking softly so that Aaron could not hear him, he said, "I was delivering the chest to the parson. He's hiding it where Mrs. Pearson won't look."

"Wise man. I'm sure he knows better than I that his wife has more than her share of curiosity." Bertha had caught Celia sewing a shirt for Mark and had demanded to know whether Hiram would also receive one. When Celia had explained that she had knitted socks for her other boarder, her friend had raised an eyebrow and chuckled.

"She's looking out her front window right now," Mark said with a wry smile. "I only hope she wasn't there half an hour ago."

Celia wondered why a simple delivery had taken so long, but she wouldn't ask. As pleasant as it was talking to Mark, she had errands to run and work to finish today, and so did he. "I doubt Bertha was at the window when you arrived," Celia told Mark. "She's probably looking for me."

As a gust of wind threatened to turn his hat into a tumbleweed, Mark gripped the brim. "That's a relief. I wouldn't want to spoil the surprise. After all, Christmas is supposed to be a time for surprises."

"My mother used to say it was the time of miracles."

Mark laughed as Emma raised her arms, demanding to be picked up. "Sorry, little one," he said, "but if I don't get back to work, I'll need a miracle to finish everything by Christmas." He waved and headed north while Celia gathered Emma and the cider into her arms and climbed the parsonage steps, Aaron by her side.

"Is that my big boy?" Bertha crouched down, extending her arms to Aaron after she closed the door behind them. "Come to the kitchen. I have something for you."

The child's eyes widened. "Sugar cookies?"

"Only if you've been good."

"I good." He looked up at Celia, his eyes imploring. "Right, Mrs. Celia?"

"Yes, you are." Celia followed Bertha into the kitchen. "You're spoiling him, you know," she said as the older woman seated Aaron at the table and placed a plate with two enormous cookies in front of him. "When I told him we were coming here, all he could talk about were your cookies."

Bertha grinned. "The boy needs some spoiling. Besides, I like pretending he's a grandchild. I figure that the good Lord had a reason for not giving me children, but he surely won't mind if I adopt a grandson."

And Aaron could use a grandmother like Bertha. "I brought you a little thank-you," Celia said, handing the towel-wrapped jar to her friend.

Bertha smiled as she unwrapped the gift, then unscrewed the lid to sniff the contents. "This smells wonderful. Thank you." She laid it on the counter out of Aaron's reach before turning back to Celia. "Now, indulge an old woman. Tell me why your boarder has been spending so much time with my husband. This is the fourth time I've seen him at the church this week."

Surely no Christmas gift required four visits. Like Bertha, Celia was curious, but her curiosity mingled with hope as she recalled Mark's changed expression.

"Maybe he just wants to talk," she suggested. "Have you asked the reverend?"

Bertha nodded. "He said it was business."

Perhaps it was.

The rest of the day proved to be as busy as Celia had expected. Without Aaron underfoot, she was able to finish sewing Mark's shirt and the rag doll she had planned for Emma. She had even started knitting a scarf and mitten set for Lionel. The promise of pound cake must have done the trick, for Mark's uncle had agreed to spend Christmas Day with them. That was part of the reason Celia wanted this Christmas to be so special. It would be Lionel's first holiday in Easton. Just as importantly, it was Emma's first Christmas ever. And, though she didn't want to dwell on the thought, it might be the only one Celia would spend with Mark. He'd said nothing more about leaving in the spring, but he'd also said nothing about staying. Since their future was uncertain, she had resolved to enjoy every moment of the present.

Supper was over; the dishes were done; everyone was gone, and so Celia returned to the parlor, her knitting in hand. If she spent another hour, she would be able to complete the first of Lionel's mittens. The needles clicked rhythmically as she transferred stitches from one needle to the next. While Mama had claimed that knitting on four needles was complicated, Celia enjoyed working her stitches in rounds, knowing there would be no seams to weave at the end. She held up the mitten and was checking the size against the pattern she had made of Mark's hand when she heard familiar footsteps.

"Are you finished for the night?" she asked when Mark appeared in the doorway.

He shook his head. "I've got another hour or so, but I needed a break. I wondered if I could have some coffee."

"Of course." Celia rose and walked to the kitchen. "There's one cup left, but it won't take long to make another pot."

While they waited for the water to boil, Mark leaned against the wall. "This is the first chance I've had to ask you if Mrs. Pearson wondered why I was at the church."

Celia nodded. It wasn't only Bertha who was curious. "She said you've been there every day this week. That piqued her interest enough that she asked her husband."

Mark's expression was inscrutable. "What did he tell her?"

When the kettle began to whistle, Celia removed it from the burner and poured the water over the coffee grounds. "He claimed it was business."

Mark chuckled and took a seat at the table. "I guess that's one way to describe it. I was there to talk about his business."

Celia felt her heart skip a beat. If Mark had indeed been consulting Reverend Pearson about his business—his real business— that would explain the difference she had seen in Mark.

"You're not talking about the blanket chest, are you?" Celia pulled two cups from the shelf and filled them.

As she approached the table, Mark's smile lit his face, turning his eyes to silver. "No. It was something infinitely more important. The parson has been ministering to my soul."

Celia sank onto the chair across from Mark and breathed in the fragrant aroma of coffee, wondering if she would ever smell it again without remembering this moment. She and Mark had shared so many confidences over cups of coffee, but nothing—absolutely nothing—could compare to this.

"It still seems strange to be talking about my soul." Though he wrapped his hand around the cup, he did not sip it. "I never really believed I had a soul, but everything changed on Sunday."

She hadn't been mistaken. The peace she thought she had seen on Mark's face was real. Celia's heart filled with joy, making her want to sing aloud.

"I feel like a piece of newly sawn lumber." A wry twist of the lips accompanied his words. "I'm rough around the edges. I know I'll need a lot of sanding and many coats of paint before I'll be ready for anything useful, but I've taken the first step."

The joy that had filled Celia's heart overflowed, spilling throughout her body, warming every inch. "Oh, Mark, I'm so happy. God has answered my prayers." He had given her a miracle.

Mark leaned back in the saddle, trying to ignore thoughts of the many gifts he had yet to make, including the ones he wanted for Emma and Celia. He ought to be in his workshop, his hands guiding a saw or a plane, not holding Charcoal's reins. But even more than he needed to be working, he needed advice. It was not something he could ask Frank or Jacob. They wouldn't help him, and Reverend Pearson was already spending a lot of time with Mark. He couldn't ask for more. That left Lionel. Though Mark wasn't sure his uncle would be able to help him, he had to try, and so here he was, approaching the cabin.

"I didn't expect you today." Lionel appeared on the top step while Mark hitched Charcoal to the wooden stake he'd driven into the ground for that express purpose. "I woulda made some stew if I knew you was coming."

Though the thought of his uncle's stew made Mark's mouth water, he shook his head. "I can't stay long, but I wouldn't refuse a cup of coffee."

Lionel grinned as he closed the door behind them. "Always got that." He reached for the pot and poured out two cups. As he walked toward the table, he nodded at the wall. "It's mighty nice havin' all the leaks fixed. This cabin's downright comfortable now." Lionel slid one of the cups across the table to Mark, picking up the other as he asked, "So, why are you here?"

There was no point in prevaricating. This was why he'd come: for advice. Mark fixed his gaze on his uncle. "You told me not to let

Celia slip away. I don't want to. I want to court her, but the problem is, I don't know how."

Lionel sputtered as he started to laugh with a mouthful of coffee. "You're askin' me? That shore is funny, comin' to a bachelor for courtin' advice." He pounded his fist on the table to punctuate his words.

"Then you can't help me?"

"I ain't said that. I ain't never done no courtin' of my own, but I heard tell how others did it. You gotta start with pretty words. The ladies like poetry and stuff like that."

But Mark didn't know any poetry except nursery rhymes, and he was pretty sure that wouldn't impress Celia. He finished his cup of coffee, listened to his uncle's tales of trapping a beaver when he'd been hoping for a rabbit, then headed back toward Easton. There was work to be done, and he had just wasted the morning. Lionel's advice might be good, but it wasn't advice Mark could use. He was back where he'd started, with no idea how to court Celia.

As he rode, Mark's thoughts continued to whirl. Maybe Lionel was wrong. Maybe words weren't the answer. Celia had been pleased when Mark had cut wood and pumped water his first night in Easton. Perhaps that was the answer. He had always believed that deeds were more powerful than words. As he led Charcoal to his stall at the livery, Mark made his decision. He would court Celia with deeds, not fancy words. And maybe, just maybe, she would understand.

Chapter Ten

"Thank you, Mark." Somehow or another he found time to fill her wood box and pump water for her, not just every evening but several times a day. Her life was much easier, since she didn't have to worry about those routine chores, but his…Celia couldn't imagine how late Mark must be staying in his workshop to make up for the time he spent helping her. "You're spoiling me."

The smile he gave her was so tender that it made her flush. Ever since his last visit to his uncle, he had seemed different. It wasn't just all the thoughtful things he did for her or the fact that he lingered after meals to share an extra cup of coffee with her. What pleased Celia most was the way Mark looked at her. He smiled more often than before. That was notable in itself, but what brought color to her cheeks was that these were not the ordinary smiles he gave to others. Instead, they hinted at secrets and sent a warm glow spiraling through her.

As she refilled his cup, Mark smiled again. "It's not spoiling. I'm just trying to help. I know you have extra baking planned for today."

With a quick glance at the calendar hanging on the opposite wall, Celia nodded. Today was December 13, St. Lucia Day. "I didn't celebrate last year," she told Mark. The combination of deep mourning for Josef and a difficult pregnancy had made last December the worst one of Celia's life. All she had wanted to do was stay in bed with the covers over her head. "I want to make up for that this year." That was why she had invited the Pearsons to join her for dinner. In return, Bertha had volunteered to keep Aaron during the day.

"I never heard of St. Lucia Day until you mentioned it," Mark said when he'd swallowed a mouthful of coffee.

"That's because you're not Swedish." Celia gave him a playful smile. "If you were, you'd know it's one of our most important winter celebrations. There are a number of stories about how it started, but most agree that Lucia was an early Christian who was martyred for bringing food to the Christians in the cata-combs of Rome. No one knows exactly what kind of food she brought them, but legend says she wore candles on her head so that her hands were free to carry a tray."

Celia nodded toward her daughter, who was playing quietly in the corner of the kitchen she had barricaded for her. "I want Emma's first St. Lucia Day to be a special one. Of course, she's too young to wear a coronet of lighted candles." A laugh escaped as Celia pictured her daughter in the traditional garb designated for the oldest daughter of each household. It would be years before Emma was old enough to follow the custom of walking through the house in her white gown and red sash, carry-ing coffee and a plate of the traditional holi-day buns. "I'd hate to see what Emma would do with a candle."

Mark's gray eyes sparkled as he joined in the laughter. "I'll bet she'd eat it, if it wasn't lit."

"Probably. In the past week or so, Emma's become curious about everything. The prob-lem is, she seems to think the only way to learn about new things is to taste them."

After draining his cup, Mark placed it on the counter next to the sink. "Will you let her taste the *lusse*…? What was it you called them?"

"*Lussekatt.*"

"Lucy cat?"

Celia nodded. "*Lussekatts* are part of the tradition. They're yeast buns flavored with saffron to make them yellow. We shape them like an *S*, so they look a bit like a sleeping yellow cat." Celia smiled as memories washed over her. Her initial attempts had borne absolutely no resemblance to cats. "Whenever I smell them baking, I remember the first year my mother let me help her make them. I was so proud."

"Before you know it, you'll be teaching Emma."

Though it was difficult to picture her daughter, who was just beginning to crawl, being old enough to place the raisin eyes on the *Lussekatts,* Celia knew the time would pass more quickly than she dreamed possible. In a few years, Emma would be able to help her, but Mark...

Resolving that she would not worry about the future, Celia fixed a smile on her face and said, "One of the reasons I like St. Lucia Day is that it's a reminder that Christmas is coming."

As if on cue, Mark rose. "The unfinished gifts in my workshop are all the reminder I need."

"I wish I could help you." Celia filled a small pot with coffee for him to take back to the workshop. Though she knew Mark didn't want to disappoint anyone, she feared he might have taken on too many commissions for Christmas gifts, and she worried that he was working too many hours.

He nodded as he accepted the coffee. "Thank you. The coffee helps keep me awake."

Even after he left, Celia continued to smile.

Each day she felt herself growing closer to Mark as she discovered new facets of his personality. He wasn't simply a skilled carpenter and a considerate boarder. He was also a man who thought deeply, who absorbed learning the way a thirsty plant did rain. Celia could admit it, even to herself. She loved Mark.

Oh, how she loved him! Though he'd never been far from her thoughts, now it seemed as if everything reminded her of him. A glimpse of blue sky brought back memories of the day he had taken her to visit his uncle. Snow reminded her of his first night here and how he'd filled the wood box and pumped water for her. Every time Celia entered the storage room, the finely crafted shelves were a testament to his thoughtfulness. And each time she made coffee, she was reminded of the night he'd revealed his renewed faith.

She loved Mark. She loved him, and she wanted nothing more than to spend the rest of her life with him. It was as simple and as complicated as that. The problem was, though she knew her own love to be deep, she did not know what Mark felt. He cared about her. That much was clear, but was it love or simply friendship? He was kind; he was thoughtful. If she let herself dream, she would say he was loving. His actions said he cared, but without the words, Celia was unsure what he really meant. She couldn't ask him. A lady didn't do that. Besides, the answer might be embarrassing for both of them. All she could do was wait and hope that one day Mark would put his feelings into words.

Mark examined the small object he'd just finished carving, turning it slowly so he could see each side. When he had examined it from every angle, he let out a sigh of relief. This was the best work he'd ever done. The question was, would she like it? Would she realize that he was offering his heart along with the gift?

After tucking Celia's Christmas present into the simple box he'd made for it, Mark crossed to the other side of the workshop and reached for the piece of pine that would soon be a crumb tray and scraper. It had taken considerable restraint not to smile when Frank asked him to make an item Celia could use on the dining table. Didn't the man realize that she wanted to be recognized for more than her cooking? When Mark had suggested a box for her gloves, Frank had been adamant. The gift had to be for the dining room.

Even though he thought Frank was making a mistake, Mark had to admit that he was looking forward to creating the crumb tray. It wasn't simply that the gift was for Celia, although that was part of the pleasure. Even greater was the feeling that carving was what he was meant to do.

As he began to saw, Mark reflected on how much his life had changed. Two months ago, he'd been an itinerant carpenter, searching for his father. And now...his search had ended. He would wander no more, and though he knew that part of his life would always be devoted to carpentry, he harbored the hope that he could make a living turning wood into items of beauty. Carving brought joy to his heart. That and Celia.

Mark brushed sawdust from the pine. It was softer wood than he would have chosen, but that was what Frank wanted. The store owner had confided that Celia's main gift would be a case of canned oysters but that he also wanted her to have something permanent, something that would remind her of him even when he was away. Mark knew that he didn't need an object to remind him of Celia. He didn't even have to be awake to think of her, for he dreamt of her almost every night.

Two months ago he had been searching for one thing: his father. But what he'd found was more than he had sought. Though he hadn't been reunited with Pa, he'd discovered the truth about his parents, and he'd met Celia. Wonderful, unforgettable, lovable Celia. Two months ago he hadn't known she existed, and now he could not imagine his future without her. Mark Williams, the man who never thought he would settle down or marry, had no trouble picturing himself spending the rest of his life in Easton.

If Celia would have him.

Mark could deny it no longer. He loved Celia with every fiber of his being. Only one question remained: Did she love him enough to trust him with her future and Emma's?

"Are you certain you don't mind?" Celia gave Mark an anxious look. He'd done so much for her that she hated to ask for more, but Emma was adamant. No one but Mark was going to carry her to the church, not even her mother.

He shook his head and reached for Emma. "The little one's no trouble."

As she wrapped her cloak around her, Celia raised an eyebrow. "We'll see if you're still saying that after the service. I don't know how she'll behave. She's not used to being up so late."

It was Christmas Eve, and though her daughter was fussing, Celia would not consider missing the services. Fortunately, once she was in Mark's arms, Emma quieted, and the walk to the church was a silent one, the only sounds the crunching of snow beneath their boots and Emma's occasional coos. Celia's parents had made it a tradition that the walk to Christmas Eve services was devoted to quiet contemplation of the blessed event they would soon celebrate, and Mark had agreed it was a wonderful custom.

"Just so you don't expect me to be quiet afterward," he'd warned Celia. "I want to be the first to wish you a Merry Christmas."

The smile he'd given her had been so tender that Celia had felt color rush to her cheeks. Would Mark say more than "Merry Christmas"? Would he say the words she dreamt of each night? She could only hope and pray.

Once they entered the sanctuary and took their places in the last pew, Celia looked around. As she had expected, it seemed as if everyone in town was there, filling the room with the scents of hair oil and toilet water, the sounds of whispered conversations and fussy children, and the almost palpable sense of excitement. The moment everyone in Easton had been waiting for approached.

When the last notes of "Adeste Fideles" faded and the congregation resumed their seats, Reverend Pearson took his place behind the pulpit. "'And it came to pass in those days...'"

As he read the familiar story, Celia's heart filled with happiness. Here she was in the church that had brought her so much comfort, with her long-awaited daughter and the man she loved. It was an almost-perfect moment. She looked down at Emma, who had finally agreed to let her mother hold her. The child was sleeping, but as Celia watched, Emma opened her eyes and reached for Mark.

"Dada." The word was soft but distinct.

Celia stared, not quite believing what she'd heard. She had never used that term around Emma, but Aaron had. Perhaps that was where Emma had learned it.

"Dada." As Emma repeated the word,

Mark stroked her cheek with his fingertip, then raised his eyes to meet Celia's gaze, giving her one of those special smiles that made her feel as if she were the only woman in the world. But this smile was different, for there was a sense of wonder in it, and the way he touched Emma told Celia that he loved her daughter as much as she did.

She had been mistaken. This moment wasn't *almost* perfect. It was perfect. The happiness that had been building inside Celia's heart overflowed, sending bubbles of joy throughout her. Even if only for a moment, for this one perfect moment, they were a family.

Celia wondered if the happiness that surged through her was evident on the outside. She felt as if she were glowing like a lantern. Though she had never failed to be thrilled by the story of the nativity, this year it had an even deeper meaning, for this was the first Christmas that she held her own child in her arms. Like Mary, she had known the pain of birth and the infinite joy of hearing her baby's first cry. She was a mother, and though Emma was only human, Celia doubted if even Mary had loved her child more.

"'And suddenly there was with the angel a multitude of heavenly host praising God, and saying, glory to God in the highest, and on earth peace, good will toward men.'" While Reverend Pearson read the timeless words, Celia closed her eyes in silent prayer. *Thank you, Lord. Thank you for my daughter, for Mark's presence in our lives, and most of all for the gift of your Son.*

As they rose for the benediction, Emma stretched her arms out to Mark. When he nodded, Celia transferred her daughter to him, watching as Emma cuddled close to the man she'd called Dada. Though Emma would not recall this moment, it was etched on Celia's memory.

"Merry Christmas." It wasn't quite midnight, but Mark seemed to be taking no chances.

"Merry Christmas, Mark." Celia smiled at him and added, "I'm glad you're here."

"Me too." They weren't the words she'd hoped for, but this was not the time or place for a declaration of love.

Celia and Mark had reached the bottom of the steps and were heading home when she heard the cry. "Mrs. Celia. Mrs. Celia." Aaron pushed his way through the crowd still leaving the church and raced toward her, tumbling down the steps and landing with his face planted in the snow. "I hurt, Mrs. Celia. I hurt."

Crouching, Celia put her arms around Aaron. Though his face might sport a bruise tomorrow, he had not broken the skin. "You'll be all right," she said softly. Then, as the church bells began to chime, she whispered, "Merry Christmas, Aaron."

The boy was once again smiling when his father reached them a minute later. As Jacob hoisted his son onto his shoulders, he looked at Celia. "He wants you to be his mother, you know."

She nodded and started to turn back to Mark and Emma, but Jacob put a hand on her arm. "I know it's still a week until New Year's, but I was kinda hoping you'd give me your answer tonight. Marrying you would be a sight easier than sending for a mail-order bride, especially since there's no telling how Aaron would take to her."

Celia shook her head, wondering whether Mark had overheard Jacob. He'd spoken softly, so perhaps he hadn't. Still, Jacob's words threatened to spoil the evening. She knew she had to make a decision, and she would, but this was not the time or place, and so Celia said only, "I need the extra week, Jacob." Before she could answer Jacob, she needed to know how Mark felt and whether her dream of happily-ever-after with him would come true. If not…

As she returned toward the boardinghouse, Celia's heart was heavy. Though he tried, it was obvious that Jacob couldn't handle his son alone. Aaron needed a mother, and Celia was the obvious choice, at least for him and his father.

She knew Jacob didn't love her. In his defense, he had never pretended that love was the reason he wanted to marry her, and his words tonight only confirmed that. Their marriage would be a business arrangement, not much different from Celia's marriage to Josef. She took a deep breath, reminding herself that that union had brought her happiness and Emma. Perhaps marriage to Jacob would be equally pleasant.

Biting back tears, Celia tried to concentrate on the beauty of the season. A light snow was falling, and for once it was not driven by the wind. Instead of icy pellets stinging her face, she felt the soft kiss of snowflakes on her cheeks. Emma was sleeping in Mark's arms, and he seemed pensive. Perhaps he was quiet because he was exhausted by the long hours he had worked to complete the townspeople's Christmas gifts. Celia didn't know. All she knew was that her heart ached.

Chapter Eleven

She tied the apron strings, then reached for the coffee. Mark would need it for his journey, and she needed it to wake up. Though she had tried to summon slumber, Celia had slept little. Instead, she had lain motionless, remembering Aaron's face when he'd run to her and trying to imagine life as Jacob's wife. Each time she had thought she knew what her answer would be, the memory of those precious moments in the church when she had felt that she and Mark were a family would resurface.

Over and over, the thoughts circled through Celia's brain, causing her to clench her fists, then force herself to relax. It was only when she abandoned all hope of sleep and began to dress that she felt the indecision that had plagued her slide away as swiftly as a sheet of ice from a steep roof, shattering when it hit the ground. There was only one answer. She could not marry Jacob. Even if it meant raising Emma alone, Celia would not tie herself to a man she did not love. She and Emma deserved more than a convenient marriage.

The coffee was ready by the time she heard footsteps on the stairway, its aroma filling Celia with happy memories, confirming that her decision was the right one. She reached for a second cup.

"Merry Christmas, Celia." His hair still wet from his morning ablutions, Mark looked more handsome than ever today. His snowy white shirt, dark jacket, and silver gray ascot were the ones he'd worn to church last night, and yet they looked somehow different today, more festive. Or perhaps it was only Celia's mood that made her imagine a difference.

"I thought you might like a cup of coffee before your trip," she said, gesturing toward the pot. The plan was for Mark to bring his uncle back to Easton for breakfast at the boardinghouse. Though Celia had suggested that Lionel come on Christmas Eve for the traditional Swedish dinner and stay overnight, he'd refused, and so she had changed her plans, moving the big meal to Christmas Day and resolving to make their celebration span the entire day.

"Coffee would be good, but there's something I want to do first." Mark looked around the room. "Is Emma still asleep?"

"Surprisingly, yes. It must have been all the excitement and the late night, but she's sleeping later than normal."

That seemed to please Mark. "I'll be right back." Without bothering to put on a coat despite the frigid temperatures, he headed for the door.

"You'll freeze," Celia said. Even worse, he might catch cold and be as ill as Emma had been. But Mark merely shook his head.

Only moments later he returned, carrying a bulky object that he'd draped with a blanket. "This is for Emma," he said as he placed it on the floor. "I know you planned to open gifts later, once Uncle Lionel and the others arrive, but I couldn't wait any longer to show this to you. I hope you'll like it."

The uncertainty in Mark's eyes tugged at Celia's heart, telling her the man she loved so dearly was vulnerable. She looked at the blanket, trying to imagine what was underneath it.

"I know Emma's too young for this right now," Mark continued, "but I had one as a child. My mother claimed it was my favorite toy for a number of years. That's why I thought Emma might enjoy one."

Slowly, almost as if he were reluctant to reveal it, Mark uncovered the gift. For a second, Celia was speechless, overwhelmed by its beauty. Then she found her voice and turned to Mark, hoping the smile that threatened to crack her face told him of her pleasure. "Oh, Mark, I've never seen anything so beautiful."

She had seen rocking horses before and had, in fact, owned one as a child. But that had been an ordinary rocking horse. This one was a work of art. Its face was so lifelike that Celia almost expected to hear it neigh, and its gently sloped back practically begged a child to climb on it. But what turned the carved animal into something truly extraordinary was the wreath of roses around its neck. Though the horse itself was simply varnished, the roses were painted red, white, and every shade of pink. While some were fully opened, others were buds just starting to bloom. Mark had created a bouquet of roses.

"This is magnificent." Celia ran her finger around one of the flowers, delighting in the detailed carving, and in that moment, she wished she were small enough to ride the horse. "It's the most beautiful thing I've ever seen. I can't imagine that the one you rode as a boy looked like this."

Mark shrugged.

"I'll bet yours didn't have roses."

He shrugged again. "That's true, but I was a boy. Little girls like different things. I know you like roses, so I thought your daughter might too."

Tears sprang to Celia's eyes at this latest evidence of Mark's thoughtfulness. Not even Josef had understood how much she loved roses, but Mark did. Emma's rocking horse was the perfect present, a gift of his time and talent, made all the more special by the thought that he had put in to designing it. He had created a toy that both Emma and her mother would treasure.

"I don't know what to say." Celia stroked the wooden horse's head before turning back to Mark. "No one has ever given me a present like this."

Mark's lips curved into a wry smile. "The horse is for Emma. You have to wait for your gift."

There had never been a Christmas like this. Mark smiled as he looked around the parlor. This had been the happiest Christmas he could remember, all because of Celia. She had made it a special day for everyone, especially Lionel.

Mark gave his uncle a quick glance, then

looked away when he saw that the man was staring at Emma, an odd expression on his face. Lionel had been quieter than normal on the ride to Easton, leaving Mark to assume that he was apprehensive about being around so many people. Celia had changed that the instant he entered the house. As soon as his uncle had shucked his coat, she had thrust a cup of coffee in his hand and led him to the parlor where Emma's rocking horse sat in front of the tree.

"Isn't it wonderful?" she asked, gesturing toward the gift. "Mark made it."

Lionel blinked and set his cup on one of the tables. Approaching the rocking horse, he ran his hands over it, tracing the outline of the largest roses. "You're a mighty talented man." Lionel's lips twisted into a wry smile. "You must have inherited that from your ma. You shore didn't get it from your pa." He was silent for a second, touching the carved garland again. "I reckon your pa'd be proud if he could see you today."

Moisture filled Mark's eyes, and he turned aside lest someone see how deeply Lionel's words had affected him. "I hope he would. I guess I'll never know, will I?" he said when he'd regained his composure.

Before Lionel could respond, Hiram descended the stairs, and Celia announced that breakfast was ready. The rest of the day passed too quickly. Frank, Jacob, and Aaron arrived for dinner and the opening of gifts, both of which showcased Celia's kindness. Though Mark knew she was short on time and funds, she had a special gift for everyone. She had made a rag doll for Emma and a stuffed horse for Aaron. If that weren't enough, she'd knitted a pair of socks for Hiram and had surprised Lionel with a warm scarf and pair of mittens. But all the gifts paled compared to the wonderfully soft flannel shirt she had made for Mark. He'd never had one that fit so well. When he'd asked her how she'd known his size, Celia had blushed slightly, telling him a benefit of doing his laundry was that she could measure his shirts.

Though Frank and Jacob looked a bit disappointed when their gifts were large tins filled with cookies, Mark had felt his spirits continue to soar as he hoped that their less personal gifts were a sign that Celia was not considering Jacob's proposal. He might be a good father—and Mark would not dispute that—but she deserved a better husband than a man who'd tell the woman he was wooing that he was also considering a mail-order bride.

For her part, Celia seemed pleased with her

gifts, oohing and aahing over Hiram's sack of candy, the crumb tray from Frank, and the linen handkerchiefs from Aaron and Jacob. Mark hoped it wasn't his imagination that her eyes held a special sparkle when she opened the rose-colored glass vase he'd given her. He didn't know what kind of flowers bloomed here, but when he'd seen the vase in Frank's store, he'd thought it would look pretty in Celia's parlor, even empty.

They'd all eaten more food than they needed, then returned to the parlor to sing Christmas carols. And now, as the sun began to set, Jacob gathered Aaron's gifts, Frank made his farewells, and Hiram climbed the stairs. Within minutes, only Celia, Mark, and Lionel were in the parlor.

"Are you certain you won't stay overnight, Mr. Williams?"

Mark's uncle shook his head. "'Fraid not. I shore appreciate the offer, ma'am, but I cain't sleep in a strange bed."

Celia nodded. "At least let me fix a basket of food for you." Without waiting for a response, she headed for the kitchen.

For a moment, there was silence in the parlor. Then Lionel approached the rocking horse, touching the garland before setting it into motion. When he turned, his eyes were glistening. "It's fine work, Mark. Your pa is mighty proud of you."

Mark shrugged, wishing his uncle hadn't brought up the subject of his father again. "I'd like to think so."

"I know so." Lionel cleared his throat and took a step toward Mark, extending his hand. "There's no way but to say it plain out. You see, son...I'm your pa."

For a second, Mark could do nothing but stare. Then, as the words registered, he felt the blood drain from his head. "You?" He grabbed the closest chair back for support. "If you're my father, why did you pretend to be Lionel? Was he the one who died?"

The older man shook his head. "I never had a brother. You shore flummoxed me the day you showed up, lookin' so much like me. I reckoned I had to come up with a story. Couldn't let you know the truth."

Anger surged through Mark. He'd traveled so far, searching for his father, and when he found him, the man lied. "Why? Why did you let me think you were dead? Why did you say my father was killed in that box canyon?"

"I almost died there." The gray eyes so like his own darkened with remembered pain. "It took months 'fore I could walk again. Bein' stuck in bed gives a man plenty of time to figger out what he oughta do with his life. I didn't want you and Grace to hold out any hopes of seein' me again. That's why I had someone send her a letter telling her I had died. I figgered she'd remarry, once you was grown. I may be a selfish old coot, but I couldn't stand thinkin' she was gonna grow old alone."

"You could have come back. We both wanted you there." Though the words were harsh, Mark felt his anger fade into regret. He wasn't the only one who had suffered. All three of them had lost so much.

"And let you see a broken man who wasn't good at anything? I didn't have much left, but I still had my pride." Clearing his throat again, he laid his hand on Mark's arm. "You may not believe me, but I love you, son. Always did. I just figgered you'd be better off without me. I reckoned I wouldn't be much of a pa, so I left." His grip tightened. "I'm sorry I hurt you and your ma, but I cain't undo that. What I wanna know is, can you forgive me?"

There was only one possible answer. As regrets faded and his heart filled with happiness that the empty years were over, Mark took a step forward and wrapped his arms around his father. "You're the best Christmas present I've ever had." Refusing to let go of the man he'd finally found, Mark turned toward the kitchen. "Celia, come meet my father."

What a wonderful Christmas it had been! Celia hummed as she washed and dried the china. Her prayers had been answered, for Mark's dream had come true. And maybe, just maybe, her own would too. Now that he'd been reunited with his father, Mark might make Easton his home.

She was putting the last dish back in the china cabinet when she heard the front door open. He was back.

"Was it hard leaving your father?" she asked as she joined Mark in the parlor. In a moment, she would offer him another cup of coffee and a piece of pound cake, but first she wanted to be certain he had no regrets about taking Abe back to his cabin.

Mark nodded. "I wish he'd move into town, but I can't complain. All that matters is that I found him. It made my day almost perfect."

"Almost?" Celia heard the astonishment in her voice. "What more could you want?"

A small smile tilted his lips upward. "Christmas isn't over yet. There's one more gift to open." Mark reached into his pocket and withdrew a small wooden box. "I know it's supposed to be wrapped, but I'm all thumbs when it comes to paper and ribbons."

Celia stared at the box. Though simple, its top was embellished with a carved *C*, leaving no doubt that it was meant for her. "It's lovely, Mark, and it's just the right size to hold my mother's string of pearls."

Mark's eyes darkened, and his voice was husky as he said, "Open it. There's something inside."

Celia paused for a second, her hands unexpectedly shaky. When she lifted the lid, her breath came out in a gasp. The rocking horse was beautiful, but this...Celia's heart raced as she stared at a perfect rosebud suspended from a golden chain. Though her brain told her that the rose was carved of wood, her heart wouldn't listen. Certain it was real, she lifted it to her nose, but instead of the sweet floral fragrance she expected, she smelled the distinctive aroma of cedar. This rose would never fade. Though Emma would outgrow the rocking horse, Celia knew she would cherish the exquisitely carved necklace for the rest of her life.

"It's beautiful," she said softly. Another tangible proof of Mark's caring, another reason not to marry Jacob. He would always have been second best, and that wouldn't have been fair to him.

Mark took a step closer. His smile faded, but his eyes gleamed with intensity. Never before had Celia seen him looking like that, both serious and tender at the same time that his eyes seemed to be asking a question. "Let me fasten it for you." When he'd secured the pendant around her neck, Mark turned her so she was facing him again. "I hope you know what this is."

"Of course. It's a rose."

He shook his head. "It's not just a rose." Reaching out, he clasped her hands. Mark's grip was warm and firm, and combined with the emotion Celia saw shining from his eyes, the simple act of joining hands made her feel cherished. That was a more precious gift than the rose itself.

"It's a Christmas rose."

A Christmas rose! Celia felt the blood rush to her face as she remembered the day she had told Mark of her fanciful wish. Afterward, she had wondered if he'd thought her foolish. It seemed he had not, for here was the proof. This wonderful man had turned one of her dreams into reality. He'd given her a Christmas rose that would never fade. More than that, he'd given her the gift of himself, using his time and talent to create the perfect present.

Mark's expression remained solemn. "You said you wouldn't marry again unless you found a man who would give you roses for Christmas."

Celia's heart skipped a beat, and in that instant, she knew the truth. Mark loved her. He might not ever say the words, but she could not doubt his love.

He tightened his grip on her hands, and smiled at her, his eyes so filled with love that Celia thought she might burst with happiness. "I know the rose isn't real, but my love is. I love you, Celia, not because you're a wonderful cook and an even better mother. I love you because you're you—a beautiful woman whose beauty is more than skin deep."

Words. He'd given her words. Warmth flooded through Celia as Mark's words filled the empty spaces deep inside her, making her wonder how she could have doubted his love. It was in his smile, in everything he did, and now it was in his touch. The hands that clasped hers were moving slowly, caressing her fingers, sending waves of delight through her veins.

He raised her hands to his lips and pressed

a kiss on her fingertips. "I love you, and I love your daughter. I don't think I could love her more if she were mine by birth."

And Emma loved him. Celia smiled as she remembered her daughter calling Mark Dada. Bertha had been right. Emma needed a father, but not just any father. She needed Mark.

"I want to be with you as you raise her. I want to give Emma a father's love." Tiny worry lines formed between Mark's eyes. "I can't promise I'll be a perfect husband or father. All I can promise is that I'll spend my life trying. Will that be enough?" Before Celia could answer, he tugged slightly, drawing her closer to him. "I love you, Celia. Will you make my life complete? Will you marry me?"

Her heart so filled with love that she feared she would be unable to speak, Celia nodded. Mark had offered her everything she had dreamt of: love, marriage, a father for Emma, and most of all, a lifetime filled with joy. They would be a family.

She swallowed deeply as she tried to form words. "Oh, Mark, I love you so much. I can't imagine anything more wonderful than being your wife."

When he bent his head and she raised her

face so their lips could touch, Celia whispered, "Mama was right. Christmas is the season of miracles."

* * * * *

REQUEST YOUR FREE BOOKS!
2 FREE RIVETING INSPIRATIONAL NOVELS
PLUS 2 FREE MYSTERY GIFTS

YES! Please send me 2 FREE Love Inspired® Suspense novels and my 2 FREE mystery gifts (gifts are worth about $10). After receiving them, if I don't wish to receive any more books, I can return the shipping statement marked "cancel." If I don't cancel, I will receive 4 brand-new novels every month and be billed just $4.74 per book in the U.S. or $5.24 per book in Canada. That's a savings of at least 21% off the cover price. It's quite a bargain! Shipping and handling is just 50¢ per book In the U.S. and 75¢ per book in Canada.* I understand that accepting the 2 free books and gifts places me under no obligation to buy anything. I can always return a shipment and cancel at any time. Even if I never buy another book, the two free books and gifts are mine to keep forever.

123/323 IDN F5AN

Name	(PLEASE PRINT)	
Address		Apt. #
City	State/Prov.	Zip/Postal Code

Signature (If under 18, a parent or guardian must sign)

Mail to the **Harlequin® Reader Service:**
IN U.S.A.: P.O. Box 1867, Buffalo, NY 14240-1867
IN CANADA: P.O. Box 609, Fort Erie, Ontario L2A 5X3

**Are you a current subscriber to Love Inspired Suspense books
and want to receive the larger-print edition?
Call 1-800-873-8635 or visit www.ReaderService.com.**

* Terms and prices subject to change without notice. Prices do not include applicable taxes. Sales tax applicable in N.Y. Canadian residents will be charged applicable taxes. Offer not valid in Quebec. This offer is limited to one order per household. Not valid for current subscribers to Love Inspired Suspense books. All orders subject to credit approval. Credit or debit balances in a customer's account(s) may be offset by any other outstanding balance owed by or to the customer. Please allow 4 to 6 weeks for delivery. Offer available while quantities last.

Your Privacy—The Harlequin® Reader Service is committed to protecting your privacy. Our Privacy Policy is available online at www.ReaderService.com or upon request from the Harlequin Reader Service.
We make a portion of our mailing list available to reputable third parties that offer products we believe may interest you. If you prefer that we not exchange your name with third parties, or if you wish to clarify or modify your communication preferences, please visit us at www.ReaderService.com/consumerschoice or write to us at Harlequin Reader Service Preference Service, P.O. Box 9062, Buffalo, NY 14269. Include your complete name and address.

LISDIR13R

REQUEST YOUR FREE BOOKS!

2 FREE INSPIRATIONAL NOVELS
PLUS 2
FREE
MYSTERY GIFTS

Love Inspired
HISTORICAL
INSPIRATIONAL HISTORICAL ROMANCE

YES! Please send me 2 FREE Love Inspired® Historical novels and my 2 FREE mystery gifts (gifts are worth about $10). After receiving them, if I don't wish to receive any more books, I can return the shipping statement marked "cancel." If I don't cancel, I will receive 4 brand-new novels every month and be billed just $4.74 per book in the U.S. or $5.24 per book in Canada. That's a savings of at least 21% off the cover price. It's quite a bargain! Shipping and handling is just 50¢ per book in the U.S. and 75¢ per book in Canada.* I understand that accepting the 2 free books and gifts places me under no obligation to buy anything. I can always return a shipment and cancel at any time. Even if I never buy another book, the two free books and gifts are mine to keep forever.

102/302 IDN F5CY

Name	(PLEASE PRINT)	
Address		Apt. #
City	State/Prov.	Zip/Postal Code

Signature (if under 18, a parent or guardian must sign)

Mail to the Harlequin® Reader Service:
IN U.S.A.: P.O. Box 1867, Buffalo, NY 14240-1867
IN CANADA: P.O. Box 609, Fort Erie, Ontario L2A 5X3

Want to try two free books from another series?
Call 1-800-873-8635 or visit www.ReaderService.com.

* Terms and prices subject to change without notice. Prices do not include applicable taxes. Sales tax applicable in N.Y. Canadian residents will be charged applicable taxes. Offer not valid in Quebec. This offer is limited to one order per household. Not valid for current subscribers to Love Inspired Historical books. All orders subject to credit approval. Credit or debit balances in a customer's account(s) may be offset by any other outstanding balance owed by or to the customer. Please allow 4 to 6 weeks for delivery. Offer available while quantities last.

Your Privacy—The Harlequin® Reader Service is committed to protecting your privacy. Our Privacy Policy is available online at www.ReaderService.com or upon request from the Harlequin Reader Service.

We make a portion of our mailing list available to reputable third parties that offer products we believe may interest you. If you prefer that we not exchange your name with third parties, or if you wish to clarify or modify your communication preferences, please visit us at www.ReaderService.com/consumerschoice or write to us at Harlequin Reader Service Preference Service, P.O. Box 9062, Buffalo, NY 14269. Include your complete name and address.

LIHDIRI3R

ReaderService.com

Manage your account online!

- Review your order history
- Manage your payments
- Update your address

*We've designed
the Harlequin® Reader Service
website just for you.*

Enjoy all the features!

- Reader excerpts from any series
- Respond to mailings and
  special monthly offers
- Discover new series available to you
- Browse the Bonus Bucks catalog
- Share your feedback

Visit us at:
ReaderService.com